Billionaires BDSM Club : Complete Collection

Lena Foxworth

DEDICATION

To everyone who ever dreamed of living happily ever
after...

CONTENTS

ACKNOWLEDGMENTS

Thank you to everyone who has made this book possible, especially the team at Reaper Moon Books.

SCARLETT

It's funny, how the biggest changes in your life happen. When you look back, you think that there should have been heavenly trumpets and bolts of lightning, but at the time, it seems so very mundane.

My life changing moment was barely perceptible when it happened. A flyer had fallen out of a magazine, one of those adverts that they seem to stuff them with nowadays. I happened to glance at it as I picked it up.

'Complete the personality questionnaire, get a free bottle of perfume.'

It was probably a scam. But the perfume looked decent enough. And it's not like I had anything for a scammer to steal. I was broke, unemployed, and unable to buy my own perfume. I checked the leaflet - yes, they'd pre-paid for the postage. What did I have to lose? I filled in the questionnaire and stuffed it in my bag. I could post it on my way to the job centre later today.

And with that act, that tiny thought of 'what do I have to lose', everything changed. I didn't even know that the downwards trajectory of my life had been irrevocably altered until three weeks later, when the perfume arrived.

I was in when the postman knocked. Of course I was in - I was always home. Nowhere to go and nothing to do. I was thrilled at receiving a package. I thanked the postman profusely, something which he didn't seem to be used to, and rushed into the living room to open it and see what on earth was inside. I'd forgotten completely about the survey at this point, so when I tore apart the packaging and discovered the perfume bottle, I was pleasantly surprised.

It was called Prism, and the bottle was a heavy, prism-shaped (well, of course) glass creation that refracted the light beautifully. It was a good size, too. But did it smell nice? I squirted a fraction onto my wrist and had a cautious sniff. It was lovely! I had a full spray then, both wrists and neck too, and let the scent envelop me. It was fabulous - rich and exotic, sensual and feminine. It smelled like the kind of scent glamorous movie stars would wear to Hollywood premiers. It smelled like first class, yachts, expensive luggage, fast cars, champagne, designer gowns. And it smelled like confidence, poise, laughter, witty repartee and seductive flirting. It smelled like the kind of life every girl dreamed of, and very, very few actually got to live.

I sat back on the couch, enjoying the feeling of being wrapped in luxury, and let my mind wander off into a daydream of living the jet-setter lifestyle. And just then, I noticed the envelope that had also been inside the packaging. It was probably an advert for the perfume, I thought as I reached for it. I was interested to know how much something like that would cost. I doubted I'd ever be able to afford to buy it, but it would be exciting to know the value of something I'd received for free.

The envelope was thick and creamy, and it had my name on the front - Elizabeth. Not printed, but hand written, with a real ink pen, rather than the cheap ballpoint pens I used myself. Hmmm, interesting, I thought as I opened it. There was a letter inside, written on the same expensive stationary in the same hand.

"Dear Elizabeth,

You are invited to attend a meeting at the Prism Club, 10 Belgrave Square, London, at 2 o'clock on Thursday. A car will be sent for your convenience."

Well, that was intriguing! I turned the paper over, looking for any more information, but there was none. A search of the packaging failed to turn anything up, either. No return address, no sender info. I wondered what in the world the meeting would be about. The questionnaire, I dimly remembered, had been a basic personality questionnaire, similar to the ones found in psychology articles. Maybe it was to recruit people to sell the perfume? If so, I was certainly interested. I badly needed the work and the income, plus the perfume smelled divine - it would sell itself.

But as a veteran of many a job interview, I knew that sales reps don't get invited to interview, not without a track record, and they don't get cars sent to take them to fancy Belgravia addresses, either. I wondered if it was dangerous. Would I wake up in an ice bath with half my organs missing? At this point, my liver and kidneys were the only thing I had left of any value. And that's when the little voice inside me spoke up again - what do you have to lose? And I knew then that if I didn't go, if I pretended to be out when the car pulled up outside my little flat, I would spend the rest of my life wondering what might have been...

I decided to accept the invitation to attend the meeting at the Prism Club.

Tuesday morning came round all too fast, and when I awoke, I was in a spin. My first issue was what to wear. How do you plan to dress when you don't know what you are attending? I was still clueless about what this meeting was regarding.

I'd googled all the information I had, which wasn't much - Prism Club and Prism perfume. Neither search had returned anything. Searching for the address hadn't revealed anything unexpected, either. 10 Belgrave Square was a large mansion in Belgravia, the most exclusive area of London and only a stone's throw from the Palace. Whatever I was dealing with, it involved money. Real money, not the facade of wealth used by scammers and individuals trying to appear they had more than they did.

I was also slightly nervous for my safety. Getting in a strange car and going to a strange place was widely considered to be a bad idea, to put it mildly. I considered telling someone where I was going, but if I was completely honest with myself, I didn't have anyone that I was that close to. I've always been the quiet, bookish type, and I've found that we often get overlooked in favour of the loud, flamboyant characters that people seem to flock to. I kept myself to myself at school, I didn't have any family to speak of, and being unemployed in a large city meant that, well, I was often lonely.

Realising this, facing it head on for the first time made me feel sad. It occurred to me that perhaps I found myself this way because I didn't take chances. I was always cautious, quiet, hiding in the shadows. It was time to change that, and an adventure into the unknown Prism Club was the perfect way to start, I decided. But just to be sure, I left the invitation clearly on display on my coffee table. If I turned the TV on, and left it with the volume fairly high, my irritable landlady was sure to investigate if it was still blaring past 10pm. I'd been late paying her this month, for the third month in a row, and tensions were at an all-time high.

I looked through my wardrobe, hoping that somehow the perfect outfit would have magically materialised out of thin air. Of course it didn't, so I was stuck with what I had. I knew that jeans weren't an option - too casual, so in the end I decided upon black trousers and a low black heel. I paired this with one of the few genuinely nice pieces I owned - a black, semi-sheer chiffon blouse with covered buttons and a ruffle detail. With a black jacket over the top, I went to the mirror to assess the result.

I was surprised - it looked better than I'd hoped. The blouse lifted the outfit from 'office manager at a funeral company' to 'mysterious, well-dressed woman'. I did a minimal make up look, and then for the final touch added a spray of Prism. Although I didn't know what was expected of me, it was pretty much a given that I'd be expected to be wearing their perfume. Finally ready, all there was left to do now was wait.

I paced the living room as the clock drew nearer to one o'clock. I'd guessed that, for a two o'clock meeting, that was the time I was likely to be collected. As I peered out of the window, a large, glossy black car turned the corner of my street and glided smoothly to a stop outside my door. This was it, then. A couple of boys approached the car - it wasn't the kind of clapped-out old banger usually seen in our street. They scurried off as a uniformed chauffeur stepped out of the driver's seat, approached the house, and rang the bell for my flat.

My heart was pounding in my chest as I locked up and headed downstairs. The chauffeur was standing by the car, and he nodded as he swept the door open for me.

"Thank you" I squeaked, as I tried to get in with as much grace and dignity as possible, as if I was collected by chauffeur-driven Bentleys every day. I doubt he was fooled.

The car's interior was a rich leather, and there was a partition separating me from the driver. Spared the daunting task of making conversation with him, I sat back and watched the roads unfold as we sped along, each street growing more and more affluent as we got nearer to our destination. At five minutes to two exactly, the car pulled up outside the Prism Club. The nerves took hold of me then, and I was frozen in my seat. That was probably a good thing, because the driver was coming round to open the door for me, and left to my own devices I probably would have clambered out before he'd had a chance to assist. I really was a fish out of water here.

He opened the car door, I stepped out, and there I was. Number 10 Belgrave Avenue. It was a large, white building. The front door was plain, revealing nothing of what lied behind it. There was no nameplate, nothing to indicate that this was the offices of the Prism Club. As I stared, the door swung open and there was another uniformed man, this one a butler.

"Miss Elizabeth."

It was a statement, not a question, but under his ultra-polite, clipped tones, there was warmth and friendliness.

"Do come inside."

I took a deep breath, and followed the butler inside.

He led me into a room that seemed to be some sort of waiting room. I perched on the leather chesterfield, hoping my nerves didn't show.

"You will be called though momentarily," he said, withdrawing.

I glanced around the room. It was tastefully decorated, with that quiet class that whispers old money, rather than the garish opulence that screams cash. There were some chairs, a coffee table, lamps. Even in my ignorance I guessed that they would be worth a fortune to an antique dealer. There was a second door, off to the side, and I guessed that was the one which I would be summoned to.

Sure enough, the door opened and an elderly woman popped her head around.

"This way please, Miss Elizabeth."

This room was an office, with a large desk dominating the area. The woman sat behind the desk, and waved a hand at the seat opposite.

"Tea, my dear?" she asked, as she began to pour from the teapot on the desk.

"Yes, please." I still felt wary, on edge. Although I didn't feel a malevolent vibe in the building, I still had no idea why I was sitting here, surrounded by wealth, while a lady in twinset and pearls poured me some tea.

She handed me a bone china cup and beamed at me.

"I expect you're wondering why you're here!"

"Well...yes...I am. Is it...to do with the perfume?"

"Yes and no. More no than yes."

She was matter-of-fact, in that confident way I so admired but always failed to emulate.

"If you recall, there was a little quiz, in order to get the perfume?"

She raised her eyebrows and I nodded.

"Well, dear, the quiz is the key to all this, you see, not the perfume. We here, at the Prism Club, we run a programme, of sorts. An advancement programme for young ladies. The quiz is just one of the many screening processes for admission to the programme."

She smiled, as if she had made it all clear and we were now at a perfect understanding of one another.

"But...but I haven't applied to join a programme."

"I know. That's not how it works. Gosh, for people to apply, we'd have to advertise it."

She said this as if advertising something was the worst possible thing that could happen.

"That would be no good, no good at all. A club like this, discretion is the key word. Discretion is what we live by. So, to find our young ladies, we go about it differently. We already know exactly what kind of person we want, it's merely a case of locating them and making ourselves known to them."

"And I...I'm what you want?"

"So far, yes." Suddenly she was all business. "The personality questionnaire indicated that you fit the psychological profile we look for. The credit checks show that you have the financial status we find works best. The background investigation told us that your social situation is ideal for the programme. The only question left now is, do you want to do it?"

I was outraged, and also embarrassed. I felt violated, that strangers had been investigating me, looking at my financial records. And embarrassed, because I knew the records would have painted a sorry story.

"Do I want to do what? Who gave you permission to...to investigate me?"

"I know it's a shock, dear." Her voice was soothing and low, and I felt some of my temper ebb away. "It's not the best way, I know, but the interview has to be the last stage of the process, after all the other things. Discretion, you see. Do you want to leave? You can if you like. I promise that we'll erase all our records of you."

Despite my anger, I didn't want to leave, and I think we both knew that. I sighed, letting go of the negativity.

"Tell me about the programme."

"I will. But first, I'll tell you about the club. The Prism Club was founded over a hundred years ago, by a group of wealthy businessmen. Gentlemen's clubs were all the rage in London at the time, but these particular men wanted something more. The Victorian era was coming to an end, and these gentlemen wanted a respite from the repression that was so common in those times. So, they founded this club, a place where they could indulge their desires with complete and utter discretion. Discretion not just for the members, but for the young ladies, too. So they created the programme. Suitable ladies would join the programme, and when they had completed it, the gentlemen would endeavour to establish the lady in society. In those days, of course, that meant a good marriage - usually to an Earl or a Duke. Although... at least one young lady of the time ended up with a HRH - the Prism Club founders were very influential within the Royal family."

She paused, refilling the teacups. I was fascinated. Who would have thought that this sort of thing had been going on for years, right here in Belgravia?

"Of course, the founding members eventually gave way to new blood. Once a gentlemen had reached a certain age, he would retire from active participation, and a replacement would be found. There's always seven, you see. No more and no less. During the war years, things were rather tough, but in the last fifty years the club has flourished. The young ladies expect different things from life now - careers, fame, fortune, that type of thing, but the gentlemen always provide it."

I felt that I was getting an understanding of what the club was about, now. Girls would entertain the men, and in return get money. Well, there was a word for that occupation!

"So, the young ladies are prostitutes, then? The members pay them for sex?"

She was horrified.

"No, no, no! The Prism Club is not prostitution. That type of thing is sex as commerce - trading one for another. The Prism Club is quite different. When a young lady enters the programme, she becomes the companion of each of the gentlemen in turn. Once she has met with all seven, they use their considerable influence to establish her however she chooses."

"But it's still sex, though."

"My dear, it is so much more than just sex. The gentlemen could get sex anywhere, after all, they're all billionaires. What they look for is a girl who will strip herself down to nothing, bare her very soul to him, allow him to remake her as he sees fit. The gentlemen are dominants and the ladies are submissive. There is sex, yes, but that's only part of the journey."

Something occurred to me.

"You said that I was suitable, that your investigation of me found that I fitted your profile. What do you mean by that?"

"Well, like I said, dear, there's three different areas that we look at. The most important, of course, is the personality profile. Not everyone is suited to being a submissive, and more importantly, to enjoy it. I'm sure there's plenty of people who'd put up with it just to get the rewards, but that's not enough. We look for people who will relish the journey of becoming a submissive, and enjoy every second of it. Your answers demonstrated that you have the personality we look for. The second area is finance. The gentlemen, as dominant, alpha males, actively enjoy transforming someone's life. It's no fun to give a reward to someone who already has the world at their feet. And the third area is social status. Joining the Prism Club means giving up everything – your home, your possessions, even your name. While you're here, you won't be Elizabeth any more, instead you'll have seven new identities, one for each member. And when you leave, you can choose to be anyone or anything you choose. Most girls decide to start completely fresh, particularly those who want to enter politics or royalty. Obviously, it wouldn't work for someone who is already well known in their community."

I felt that that was an amazingly discreet way of saying I was broke and had no friends, but then, the

Prism Club was all about discretion.

She patted my hand.

"I know it's a lot to take in. Go home, and decide. We'll send the car for you again tomorrow morning. If you decide against it, you'll never hear from us again. You can go about your life just as you have done so far. If you decide to join us, the car will bring you here and your new life will begin immediately. We'll take care of wrapping up your old one. It's entirely up to you. All you need to ask yourself is this – what do you have to lose?"

The journey home was a blur. It was indeed a lot to take in. I let myself into my tiny flat. It seemed particularly shabby compared to the beautiful building I'd come from. I checked the answering machine – no messages. I had no job, no friends, no money, nothing. So, for that part, the decision seemed to be obvious. But what about the sexual element to it? I had virtually no sexual experience. I was still a virgin, and it looked like I was going to remain that way for quite some time. So I certainly had no hands-on experience of being a submissive, BDSM, any of that. I knew what it was, though. Their personality profile had been spot on there. I'd read books about it, watched films and looked on the internet, and something about the whole thing really turned me on. I'd never been sure if it was just the idea of it that I liked though, rather than the actuality.

But then that phrase came into my mind again, the one that I kept asking myself. She'd used it, too. What have you got to lose? I knew then. When the car pulled up tomorrow morning, I would be getting in it, and starting my new life.

It was easier than I had thought, walking away from it all. As I locked my door for the last time, the hatchet-faced landlady passed me in the corridor, and gave me a sour-faced look. I realised that I would never see her again, and I was glad. The journey to Belgravia seemed to take no time at all, and before I knew it, I was passing through the unassuming front door for the second time in twenty four hours. But this time, it was for good.

The butler escorted me into the same office as yesterday, and the lady was waiting for me, smiling.

"Welcome, dear. You've made the right choice, I'm sure of it. Now, today we'll get you settled in and prepared. First things first, though - I need you to sign this form."

The form that she offered me was long and filled with legalese.

"What is it?" I asked.

"Just a standard non-disclosure agreement. The people you will meet here guard their reputations most fiercely, and of course..."

"Discretion," I finished for her.

"Yes, exactly." she beamed at me.

I signed my name at the bottom of the paper. It was done - I was in.

"Now that you're all squared away - names." she said.

It occurred to me that I had absolutely no idea what she was called. In the whirlwind of yesterday, I'd never thought to ask, and I was pretty sure she hadn't volunteered it, either.

"My name is Rose Templeton. You can call me Rose."

"Thank you, Rose. I'm Elizabeth." I said, half-jokingly.

"Not any more, you're not. For this period, your name is Scarlett."

"Scarlett?"

"Yes. During your time with each gentleman, you will become a new person for him. The first gentleman is always Mr Red - not his real name, of course - and you will be Scarlett. You are only to use that name in conversations, introductions, correspondence. You must shed Elizabeth and embody Scarlett. Now, John will show you to your quarters, Scarlett. From there, you'll be called to preparation in an hour or so."

The door opened and the butler, who was presumably named John, gestured for me to follow him. As I followed him through the house, I realised just how enormous it was, far bigger than it appeared from the road. Corridors branched off right and left, each lined with rows of doors. I wondered what could be behind them, and yearned to explore. Finally we halted outside a door with a discreet card holder attached. The card read 'Scarlett'. I was quietly relieved that my room was labelled - I had no hope of finding it again in this warren. John opened it, ushered me in, and departed, closing the door quietly behind him.

I looked around my new home. There was a huge four-poster bed, with white linen bedding. It looked like a giant cloud, and even though I wasn't in the least bit tired, I could have easily climbed in and dozed off. There was a dressing table with a mirror, and a selection of make-up arrayed on the top. I picked up a lipstick and examined it - it was a quality brand, much more expensive than I would have ever bought for myself.

Two doors led off from the bedroom. The first proved to be a bathroom. There was a claw-footed bathtub, separate shower, sink and toilet. Fluffy towels and bathrobes hung from a row of hooks along one wall. Again, all the soaps and shampoos were high-end, luxury products. I thought about my old tiny, grotty bathroom and laughed out loud with joy.

The other door led to a fully stocked closet. At first I thought the clothes must belong to a previous occupant, but then I noticed that everything was brand new, and all of it was my size. I was impressed with how thorough the club had been. Like a child on Christmas morning, I rummaged through my new swag. It was all very different to what I was used to. There were elegant dresses, long sweeping woollen coats, and shiny high heeled shoes. But the bulk of the items were lingerie, I realised. Filmy negligees, lacy bras with matching knickers, silky stockings with seams running up the back.

Seeing all the lingerie, beautiful as it was, reminded me why I was here. I wondered what 'Mr Red' would be like. Oh god, I hoped he wasn't old and disgusting. That was the trouble with really rich men, often it took them the better part of a lifetime to accumulate such wealth.

My thoughts were interrupted by a knock on the door. I opened it to find a woman, perhaps in her early forties, standing there. She was elegant and beautifully put together.

"Hello, Scarlett. My name is Davina. I'm here to help you get ready."

I stepped aside to allow her to enter, all the time fighting the instinct to correct her 'Scarlett' to 'Elizabeth'.

"Get ready?"

"Yes. You're headed for the preparation room in a little under an hour, and we need to get you decent before then. Chop chop!"

Decent? What did she mean? I thought I looked presentable enough - I mean, I'd made an effort after seeing how posh the place was yesterday.

Just under an hour later, I was beginning to get a greater understand of what 'decent' actually meant. Davina, without a hint of shame or embarrassment, had stripped me naked, tossed me into the shower ("No time for a bath, Scarlett!"), and scrubbed me to within an inch of my life. Then she'd produced a waxing kit and proceeded to remove every single hair on my body that was south of my eyebrows.

I was shocked by this, not just by the notion of having a complete stranger tearing out my hair by the roots, but also because I'd never really done much with my pubic hair before. When I pulled on the white lace underwear she'd ordered me to wear, I could feel the fabric moving against my sex in a way that I'd never experienced before. It was a good feeling, erotic and sensuous. It made me aware of every movement that I made. I was snapped out of my reverie by Davina manhandling a white satin slip over my head and pronouncing me ready.

I looked in the mirror. She'd applied the same type of minimalist make-up I usually wore, but somehow she'd managed to make it look like I was a natural, bare-faced beauty. With my hair hanging down in soft waves, and the slip floating wispily over bare feet, I looked like an innocent angel.

"Perfect." she said. "Follow me."

The thick carpet was soft under my feet as I hurried to keep up with her long strides. It felt strange, to be so casually dressed in a strange place, but I suppose 10 Belgrave Square was my home now, and I had often gone barefoot at home before. Davina opened a door and practically shoved me inside, before disappearing off like a well-dressed tornado. I got the impression it took a lot of energy to be Davina.

The distraction of Davina's exit meant that I hadn't really looked up as I entered the room, so I had practically reached the desk before I realised that the person already present was not another of the Prism Club's female employees.

The man behind the desk was older than me, probably mid-forties. He was tall, dark haired, and tanned. His well-cut suit accentuated his lithe, muscular build. I don't know if was the discreet Rolex on his wrist or just the air of power that surrounded him, but suddenly I realised that this was not just another staff member. This was one of the billionaire members of the club. And from the subtle flash of colour in his tie, it had to be...

"Mr Red?"

He smiled, revealing perfect teeth.

"That's correct. And you are Scarlett." It was a reminder, not a question.

"Have a seat. You look lovely, by the way. Davina is very...strident for my tastes, but there's no disputing that she knows exactly what she's about."

"Thank you," I said, sitting.

I was trembling with nerves. Was he going to expect me to just have sex with him, right now in this office? Another thing was nagging at my brain, too. He looked familiar. Not familiar in the sense of someone I had met, but familiar from seeing his pictures in the newspapers. Suddenly it came to me. If I wasn't very much mistaken, this man, 'Mr Red', owned a group of retail companies comprising almost half of the clothes shops on the British high street. He wasn't just lottery-winner rich, he was '100 richest men in the world' rich. I sensed it would be a faux pas to acknowledge that I knew him. Discretion, of course.

"Now, today is just to establish some ground rules, some boundaries as it were. It's always better to get this type of thing out of the way before the moment is at hand, don't you agree?"

"Absolutely," I replied, even though I had no idea what he was talking about.

"Now..." he was smiling, looking right into my eyes, and I felt the first prickle of arousal. He was a handsome, compelling man. The thought of having all his attention focusing on me was a heady experience. I tried to concentrate as he continued to speak.

"Although we looked into your affairs, we don't know everything there is to know about you."

He produced what looked like, from my upside-down perspective, to be a checklist.

"A few questions. Are you a virgin?"

I blushed. "Yes."

He made a mark on the paper, and then a few more, muttering to himself "Don't need that, don't need that one..."

"What is the nature of your sexual experience?"

"Excuse me? I don't understand." I said.

"How far have you gone?" he said kindly.

"Oh, er...not very far. Just kissing, and...erm...some touching. Over-the-clothes touching."

In actual fact, the furthest I'd ever gone with another person was when Davina viciously waxed me earlier, but I didn't think that was exactly what he was getting at.

"Do you masturbate? Hand, dildo, vibrator, other?"

The bluntness of such an intimate question shocked me into replying. "Just hand".

He seemed pleased with my answers so far.

"That's good, Scarlett. My own personal preference is for girls who haven't had much experience. Now, one more thing that we need to establish. Do you know what a safe word is?"

I thought I did, after all I wasn't completely ignorant, but I figured it was better to hear his definition of it.

"I'm not sure."

"One of the things a dominant like myself does is to push the boundaries of the submissive. An inexperienced girl like yourself doesn't know what she likes and what she doesn't like until she tries it, but it would be terribly wrong to force something on her that she doesn't want to do. So, we use safe words. If you are feeling uneasy about something that is happening, say the word One. If you are uncomfortable, the word Two. If you are in distress and need to stop immediately, the word Three. If your mouth is full, fingers or blinking is fine to use instead. I will of course obey you - it's important to me that you enjoy this just as much as I do."

He touched my arm, and I could see that he was being perfectly sincere.

"Until tomorrow, then."

He kissed me, gently on the lips, and again I felt that thrill of anticipation.

"Until tomorrow," I replied.

I was pleased to discover that I could remember my way back to my room. Getting lost in this place on my first day would be so embarrassing. I rounded a corner and bumped smack into a young man rushing the other way!

"Oooh! Sorry!" I gasped.

"No problem, love." He grinned, and pushed a sheaf of golden blonde hair out of his blue eyes. He was casually dressed, in jeans and a t shirt, and was so far the youngest person I'd met here. I wondered if the Prism Club members enjoyed boys as well as girls, but he didn't strike me as gay. He probably just worked here, maybe in the kitchens or something.

"What's your name?" he asked.

"Elizabeth." I said without thinking. "No! Wait, Scarlett. My name is Scarlett."

"Scarlett, huh?"

His voice was richly toned, like honey.

"Well, I guess I'll be seeing you around, Scarlett." He emphasised the 'Scarlett', mocking the way I'd answered with my real name. "You need to be careful with that name thing. They don't like it if you get that wrong. Discretion, and all that. Nobody uses their real name here."

"What's your name, then, since you know mine?" I said.

He leaned forward, so that his lips were next to my ear. I felt very aware of how tall he was, how wide his chest was. He smelled like citrus and I felt a sudden, uncontrollable urge to lick his neck.

"James," he whispered, "But don't tell anyone..."

He smiled devilishly and continued on his way, leaving me blushing and stuttering in his wake.

Back safely in my room, I thought about what was going to happen tomorrow. Davina had obviously been in - there was a pile of clothes stacked neatly on a chair and a note instructing me to wear them tomorrow. I noticed that my old clothes, the ones I'd arrived in, were gone, and figured that Davina had probably burned them for crimes against style.

As I lay in bed, I tried to picture being with Mr Red, sexually. He was extremely attractive, there was no doubt about that. But somehow my thoughts kept turning to James, the mysterious stranger in the corridor. I rolled over in the comfortable bed and drifted off to sleep.

It was Davina who escorted me to the room where I was to entertain Mr Red.

"Are you nervous?" she asked me as we walked along the corridor.

I was, of course I was. I was about to lose my virginity to a famous billionaire with a taste for BDSM. I was dressed in a similar outfit to yesterday - the innocent girl look. I think Davina was feeling sympathetic to my nerves, or at least trying to soothe them, because we were strolling along, rather than barrelling down the corridors at her usual brisk pace.

"Yes, I am pretty nervous," I admitted. "But kind of excited, too."

"That's good, that's what I felt when I was in your shoes."

This surprised me.

"You were one of the girls?"

"It's a long story. I'll tell you another time. For now,

you just need to focus on today."

"Do you have any tips?" I asked.

"You don't really need any, to be honest. He likes to take the lead, and he likes girls without too much experience, so just go with it. He's a good, decent man - he won't abuse his position. It's okay to use the safe words if you need to, but don't go overboard. Be honest about what you're feeling. If it's mildly uncomfortable, then flag it as that. I'd be surprised if you need to pull the plug."

I was comforted by her description of him as a good man. Part of me had been terrified about him turning out to be a crazy sadistic murderer, or something.

"Will I see you later?" I said.

"Yes. I'll collect you when you're done, take you back to your room, and look after you. It can sometimes feel a little weird after a session - but I'll make sure you're OK."

I was pleased. I knew it was her job to do these things, but it felt like I was making a real friend. We had reached a door, marked simply 'Red'.

"This is where I leave you," she said.

Suddenly, she gave me a hug.

"Relax! You'll enjoy it, I promise."

And with that, she was off again. I knocked on the door, and heard Mr Red's voice.

"Come in."

As I walked into the room, my legs felt like jelly, but I did my best to disguise my nerves. The room was themed - red, of course. A deep, blood red that was very ominous and masculine. There were various pieces of furniture scattered around the room and I looked at them, too nervous to meet his gaze. From hidden speakers, music was playing - some sort of opera. I didn't know which one.

There was a padded leather bench, what looked like

stocks, and a table with restraints at each corner. A shelf on the back wall held a variety of sex toys - dildos of varying sizes, whips and paddles, and a host of other things I didn't immediately recognise.

"Scarlett."

I raised my eyes and looked directly at him. He was bare chested and barefooted, wearing only a pair of black jeans. It made him seem more human, more approachable than when he was wearing the expensive suit, and I was able to appreciate just how attractive he was. The expression on his face was unreadable - not friendly, but not stern either.

"Take off your clothes. All of them."

He folded his arms and waited. I slid the straps of my slip over my shoulders and let it fall to the floor. Now I was only wearing my underwear. I unhooked the bra as he watched closely, and shrugged it off. The urge to cover myself was overwhelming, but I knew that it was pointless. He was going to be seeing everything. It wasn't that I was embarrassed about my nakedness, but the setting made me uncomfortable. The way he was standing, watching from across the room, made me feel more vulnerable than if I was stripping off on a crowded street. I edged my knickers down my thighs, and then I was naked.

I held my hands by my side as he stared, walking towards me. This was the first time a man had ever seen me naked, and I started to wonder what I looked like though his eyes. Was I sexy? I had no idea.

He stroked my face gently.

"Are you nervous?"

"Yes." I said.

"Don't be. I'll take good care of you, I promise. You have a beautiful body, and I intend to explore it thoroughly."

He slipped a piece of fabric out of his pocket and

moved to stand behind me. It was a blindfold. He covered my eyes, and I could see nothing. My other senses strained, trying to work out what would happen next. I jumped as I felt his hand graze the small of my back, his fingers warm to the touch.

"Come over here. Let me lead you," he said, taking my arm and guiding me forward. I was already so disorientated that I didn't know where in the room we were. Under his breath, he was humming along with the music. I felt his hands on my wrists, bringing them together behind my back, and then there was a sensation of cold metal, as if I was wearing two bracelets. I went to move my arms apart and found I couldn't - I was handcuffed.

He laughed.

"No, no. You won't escape these, I'm afraid."

Having my arms in that position was pulling my shoulder blades back, causing my breasts to thrust forward. I felt his hands caress them, the nipples hard under his touch. I was becoming increasingly aroused, and yearned for him to touch me more, all over my body, but instead I felt a sharp pain on each nipple. I gasped.

"Nipple clamps. They're attached with a chain. When I tug on it like this..."

He must have tugged the chain, because I felt another sharp pain. It was both uncomfortable and pleasurable, and I cried out.

"One more thing. Bend forward."

He guided me as I leaned, and I realised that I must be facing the table with the restraints. Unable to use my hands, I was bent at the waist, lying on my front. The nipple clamps dug into my flesh cruelly. I felt his hands on the curve of my ass, and wondered if this was it, if he was going to take me then and there. I knew that my pussy was getting wet. Could he see how much I wanted it?

To my shock, he started to finger my asshole, not my pussy. His fingers felt slick, and I realised that he must be using lube. Something hard pressed against the entrance to my hole.

"It's not my cock," he said. "It's a buttplug. Only a small one. Just relax..."

Relaxing was out of the question. The pressure increased until I thought I wouldn't be able to take it any more, and then something gave way and the buttplug slid into my ass. It was cold, and it felt huge. He put his hand around my neck and lifted my torso so that I was upright again, and then he span me round. I could feel the plug every time I moved, and I tried to grip it so that it wouldn't fall out. His hand was still on the back of my neck.

"Get on your knees."

I knelt down before him, and heard him unzip his jeans. I couldn't see it, but I knew it was there. His hard cock, right in front of my face. My first blow job. The head of his cock touched my lips, and I was surprised at how soft the skin was.

"Lick the head."

I started to lick it as if it were a lollipop, swirling my tongue around it, and I heard him stifle a groan. For all his stony-faced, blunt orders, he was enjoying this. I felt his hands wrap themselves into my hair, and he started to slide into my mouth, each time going a little deeper. I sucked, matching the rhythm of his motions, and his grip tightened. Then he started to pick up the pace, and his thrusts were deeper, his cock hitting the back of my throat. I was finding it harder to breathe, and spit was running down my chin.

"Oh yeah...that's it..."

I was choking and spluttering as he face-fucked me, the chain on my nipples bouncing as my body shook.

My face was pressed against his crotch as he shoved himself all the way down my throat. He groaned, and my mouth was flooded with his cum. It was hot and salty. He withdrew his cock and I swallowed as much as I could, but I could feel it dripping onto my stomach and legs.

"Did you enjoy that?" he asked.

I had enjoyed it, as rough as it had been.

"Yes," I said, and my voice was hoarse.

"Good."

He gripped my forearms and led me across the room. I felt something bump the top of my thighs, and realised it was the padded bench. Again, he lowered me forward, less gently this time. It was lower than the table had been, and my ass was pointing up into the air. I was aware of the buttplug in this new, vulnerable position.

He fumbled at my head, and I felt him push something into my mouth - a ball gag.

"Now, feel free to make as much noise as you want."

For a moment, there was nothing at all. All I could hear was the music playing. I didn't know where he was or what he was doing. Then...WHACK! He had slapped me, hard, on the cheek of my ass. I cried out and the gag muffled the sound.

"That's right...let me know you feel it..."

His hand came down again, this time on the other cheek, and I yelled once more. A flurry of slaps came then, too many to count. With each one I could feel the butt plug move. I screamed through the gag, enjoying the way I was able to completely let go - it felt almost primal. And then, his fingers were on my pussy. I was soaking wet, and he massaged my clit, rubbing back and forth but never penetrating me. His other hand continued to spank me, but between the screams I was moaning with pleasure. Just as I felt an orgasm building he pulled away, leaving me squirming with frustration and longing.

He dragged me across the room once more, removing the handcuffs as we went. I could feel a sense of urgency coming from him. My hands were pulled forward, and then restrained once more. I was in the stocks. He stroked my ass cheeks, which were stinging from the spanking he had delivered. Then I felt the pressure of the buttplug increase and withdraw, as he removed it. Something touched my hole, and I knew that this time, it was his cock.

He took it slowly, sliding himself into my ass. He was much bigger than the buttplug had been, and I felt my asshole stretching to accommodate him. One of his hands grabbed the hair on the back of my head, pulling it up and back. The other must have been holding the nipple chain, because I felt the painful tug once more.

"Brace yourself," I heard.

And with that, he started to fuck me. That is what it was. Not sex, and certainly not making love. This was an all-out ass pounding. I was screaming out as he battered me relentlessly, the pleasure and pain all mixed up in my head until I wasn't sure one ended and the other began. Then he withdrew, and I felt another buttplug, a much bigger one, fill my aching hole. And then...nothing.

I was waiting for him, every nerve ending tingling, but it didn't come. Blindfolded, gagged and strapped into the stocks, I had no way of knowing what was happening. A minute passed, then two.

"Beg."

His voice was right in my ear. I began to plead, although the gag was reducing my words to garbled sounds. In that moment, I was desperate for him to touch me, desperate for release. I'd been turned on and wet forever. I needed him inside me. And then I felt his hands on my hips, as he guided his cock into my virgin pussy. I felt something tear as he forced his way in, and the girth of the butt plug made his cock feel impossibly large. He started to fuck me again, and almost immediately I could feel my climax emerging from the pain. I screamed, thrusting my hips back against him, wanting him to go faster, harder. As the wave broke inside me, I was vaguely aware of his cock twitching, spurting its seed inside me, but I was somewhere else entirely. Wave after wave of pleasure tore through my whole body. It was like being struck by lightning and then set on fire, and I never wanted it to end.

But eventually it did, and I floated back down to earth, suddenly aware of how utterly exhausted I was. I was trembling as he removed the buttplug, and I nearly fainted when he removed the nipple clamps. He released me from the stocks, and then finally took away the gag and blindfold. The light stung my eyes after being in the dark for so long.

"You did well, Scarlett," he said. And with that, he turned and left the room. I suddenly felt like crying. I was standing there, naked, covered in sweat with cum tricking down my thighs. But then Davina came in, carrying a huge fluffy robe. She wrapped it around me tenderly.

"He's pleased," she said. "That's good, he's not always pleased. Did you enjoy it?"

"Yes...yes I did," I said, realising as I said it that it was true - I had enjoyed it.

"Come on with me, now. I've ran you a lovely hot bath. You must be exhausted." she said, ushering me along.

"Will I be doing this again tomorrow?" I said. "I don't think I can. I'm aching everywhere."

"Oh no, you're finished with Mr Red now. That's all he's into – virgins."

"So, what happens next?"

"For the next few days, nothing. We'll just hang out

and enjoy ourselves." she said. "And then, you'll meet Mr Purple. He's great fun. Very...social."

"Will I still be Scarlett?"

"Scarlett is gone. Your name..." she paused, smiling, "is Violet."

VIOLET

It was my first full day as Violet. I'd slept solidly the night before, exhausted by my encounter with Mr Red. Davina woke me around ten, and we gossiped about everything and nothing over breakfast. It was nice to have a friend in this strange place. I was enjoying myself, but in a way the whole experience would have been quite isolating without her.

"So, Davina," I said. "You hinted yesterday that you've done all this before. How come you stayed? What about the fabulous riches and amazing lifestyle? I want to know everything about it!"

She smiled sadly, and gazed down at her feet.

"It's true, I was once in your shoes. It was a few years ago, though. Some of the gentlemen were different. Some were the same ones that are here now. I enjoyed it, the process. But then..."

She trailed off, unwilling to say more. I was intrigued. What had happened to stop her enjoying it?

"Davina, please! You can't say that and then not tell me. You're scaring me! What could have possibly happened?"

Her eyes widened in alarm.

"No, no, it wasn't like that. Nothing bad happened. You mustn't worry. It was just...I developed feelings for one of the gentlemen. Romantic feelings. And after that, it was hard to carry on through the process. We talked about it, and it was decided that I could stay at the club, doing, well, this."

She gestured around the room.

"And that's my life now. I have quarters here - this place is my home. I guide the girls through the process. I live quite well, I'm paid for what I do. But not as well as you will..."

I was relieved that there wasn't some sort of nasty surprise coming up.

"And what of the man you had feelings for?"

"He...he didn't feel the same. It was difficult, at first, living here, helping the girls, knowing that they were going to be with him. I was jealous. But eventually it got easier. He's gone now, though. He left the club a few months ago. They've only just replaced him, actually."

"Would you do it again, now that he's gone? Go through the programme again?"

"I wouldn't, but that doesn't matter. They're good about taking care of the girls who drop out, but they don't offer a once-in-a-lifetime opportunity more than once."

Well, that made sense. I felt bad for her, though. It must be hard, to be so close to what you want without being able to have it. I wanted to lift the sombre mood that had suddenly fallen on the room.

"So, tell me about the gentlemen, the ones that are here now. Dish the dirt!"

She brightened up.

"Well, obviously you met Red. Did you recognise him?"

"Did I recognise him? I was wearing one of his jackets when I came here!" I said, laughing. "Is that really all he's into, virgins?"

"Yes. Just virgins. I don't know about his personal life, but in the club he's never slept with anyone more than once."

She leaned forward confidentially.

"One time, a girl came here who'd had hymen replacement surgery. It turned out that she'd had a boyfriend and lied about it. It got missed on the background checks, too. Nobody realised, but he knew straight away. There was hell to pay after that, and she got kicked out without a penny."

"No! That's so bad. Imagine having that surgery. I mean, god, do they just sew it back up?"

We were both laughing, trying to picture what exactly went on in a hymen replacement surgery. The thought of it made me wince - I was still sore after yesterday's encounter.

"You should ask number four - Dr Blue," she said. "He's really a doctor, it's not just an affectation. That's what he's into - medical play. Obviously he could never do anything like that out in the real word, he'd get struck off. So he comes here instead. He does my Botox, too."

She wiggled her eyebrows at me, and I was impressed to see the way her forehead barely moved.

"What about the others?"

"Hmm, let's see. Number five - Green - is hugely into porn. Films, mostly, but sometimes pictures too. Don't worry, they'll disguise you enough that you won't be recognised. He's a really nice guy - in the real world he heads up a movie studio. If that's where you want to go after here - Hollywood - he's the man that will make it happen for you."

"I haven't really thought that much about what comes after, to be honest. There's so much to choose from, so many possibilities."

"There's no rush. It's not like you have to decide right away. But the ones that do go that way, let's just say they do very well..."

She named an actress, and I gasped. This woman was one of the most famous faces in the world. She'd won an Oscar, married a movie star, divorced him, married another, and obtained a car-full of children.

"She...she was here?"

"She certainly was. You'd be surprised. But that's the way it works. Girls come here as nobody - no offence - and then they become huge."

I wasn't offended. It was true, after all. I was excited by the possibilities ahead, though.

"Obviously, Mr Red is your man for business, if that's where your heart lies."

I didn't think it was, really. I couldn't get excited about board meetings and shareholders, no matter how much money and power was involved.

"I don't think so. Who else is there?" I curled up in my chair, tucking my feet gingerly beneath me.

"Can you sing? Do you want to sing?"

I warbled out the first thing that came into my head - Happy Birthday.

"OK, OK, you can't sing!" she laughed. "But I don't think that really matters. Number three, Mr Yellow, owns a record company. If you want to be an international pop star, he'll get you there. He's a very kinky man - he likes public humiliation and exhibitionism. Which will work well with your singing voice!"

I threw a cushion at her.

"Who else?"

"Mr Purple is a media mogul."

"I have literally no idea what that even means."

"News, basically. Newspapers, TV news channels,

that kind of thing. He helps girls become journalists, TV anchors, that type of thing."

"You said he was social?"

"Yes. If this was the seventies, he'd be called a swinger. He likes the clubs - group sex, orgies, gang-bangs."

I felt a prickle of excitement in my belly. This was the gentleman I would be meeting in two days' time. It seemed crazy, going from being a virgin to a swinger in less than a week, but at the same time it was exhilarating.

"Let's see, who's left? Mr Orange - I don't know him that well. He's the new one, the one that replaced...well, he's new. He's the resident nerd - he made billions from apps and games. His sexual preferences are listed as office play - the boss/secretary dynamic. But you'll be his first girl, so I don't know all that much about him. He's number six, so it will be a while yet."

I realised that Davina must have got nearly to the end before she fell in love. What a sad way for it to end.

"And finally, there's Sir Pink."

"Sir? Sir as in 'master' or Sir as in 'knight of the realm'?"

"Sir as in both, actually. He's the man who arranges good marriages. If you fancy being a Lady, he can make it happen for you. But he's...difficult to please."

"What do you mean?"

"He's always the last one the girls see. I never got as far as him, obviously, but he was here in my time. He demands total, 24/7 submission. It's not the easiest thing in the world. The drop-out rate is higher for him than for all the others put together."

That seemed a pity - of all the futures Davina had mentioned, a life of nobility was the most exciting. And it would be just awful, to get that far and then fail.

"I want to succeed at this, Davina," I said. "Will you

help me, help me with him?"

She placed her hand on mine.

"Of course I will. I'm here for you all the way. But first, we'll get you ready for Mr Purple."

The next day or so passed in a blur of preparation. For this assignation, I would be leaving the club. The thought of going out into the world seemed exciting and strange, as if I'd been away for years rather than days. I wondered if I would see anybody that I knew, but Davina reassured me that wouldn't happen.

"You will travel with Mr Purple to the venue in a blacked-out car! What did you think - that you'd be taking the tube?" she laughed.

It was true that this world of wealth and privilege was still taking some getting used to.

"But what about at the venue? How many people will be there?"

"Quite a few. They generally attract between fifty and a hundred guests. But don't worry - I guarantee you won't have met any of them before. The entrance fee is deliberately set high, it's always thousands of pounds. Most of the guests are from Europe or the States. Events like this are a big deal for a...certain set. And of course, there's one more thing..."

She opened a box, reached inside, and brandished a handful of masks.

"It's an extra layer of anonymity, just to make everyone feel safe and relaxed. Plus they add something - an air of mystery and eroticism, don't you think?"

I did think so, yes. The masks were beautiful - a real work of art. They all covered the eyes and upper face, but beyond that each one was different. There were velvet ones, soft lace, butter-soft leather, everything I could imagine and more besides.

I tried one on, a black piece with glossy feathers

stroking up towards my temples. It was comfortable, and not at all intrusive. I looked in the mirror, expecting to see a Halloween costume, but that was not the girl who started back at me. It made me look erotic, sensual, mysterious. The eye holes were cut to enhance the natural shape of my eyes, making them look bigger and somehow more exotic. I loved this!

"Which one will I wear?"

"Which ever goes best with your outfit, of course! The theme is 'dress to impress', and I don't think we'll have any trouble there," Davina said.

She had a second box, much larger, filled with outfits. They were somewhere between lingerie and evening wear - not as explicit as lingerie, but at the same time not something that you could wear to go shopping. I pictured myself on the tube in one of these creations and laughed.

After trying on everything Davina had, I settled on a black number. It had a fitted bra top embroidered with feathers, and from that, semi-sheer black chiffon floated down to the top of my thigh. Matching knickers protected my modesty, although not much. I rounded it off, of course, with the very first mask, the one I had fallen in love with.

"Perfect!" Davina pronounced, hugging me in delight. "Now, we still have a few hours. Let's get your hair and make-up done, and you'll be all ready to go."

Two hours later, I was ready. I looked at myself in the mirror. Davina was an artist. Instead of the innocent, fresh faced look she'd done previously, she'd gone for the full on seductress. My eyes were smoky and sensual, my lips full and red. My hair fell down my back in soft waves. As I gazed into the mirror at this new version of myself, I felt different. Sexy, powerful, tantalising. The kind of woman who could walk into a room and have every eye turn to her. I liked it - no, I loved it!

Davina jumped up from the couch. "It's time! I'll go and arrange the car. You go down to the lobby - he'll be waiting for you there. You know where it is, right?"

I did. I was getting better at negotiating the maze of rooms and corridors. We left my room, and she rushed off in the opposite direction. I had to proceed more slowly - the shoes I was wearing were perilously high.

I picked my way down the corridor, until I reached the stairs. Now, here was a challenge. The staircase was marble, and swept majestically down to the ground floor. I knew that one tumble on it would be dangerous and painful. Should I take the shoes off and descend barefoot? Suddenly I felt less like the powerful, sexy woman and more like my old, awkward self.

"Having a little trouble, are we?"

I jumped at the sound of the rich, masculine voice. It was James, appearing from nowhere right behind me.

"Er, yes. I'm not really used to these shoes," I stammered, blushing.

"Here," he said, and before I could even think about objecting, he had swept me up into his arms effortlessly. He strode confidently down the staircase.

"You look good. You're going out, tonight?" he asked.

"Yes," I squeaked into his chest. What was it about this man that turned me into jelly?

As we got to the bottom, there was a man standing in the lobby, staring at us. His eyes narrowed as James approached him, still carrying me.

"Thank you?" the man said, raising his eyebrows.

James set me back on my feet.

"Any time."

He squeezed my arm gently, and sauntered off.

The man watched him go, and then shook his head, turning his attention to me. He grinned, and I relaxed a little, feeling the momentary tension in the air melt away.

"You must be Violet. Shall we?"

He offered me his arm, and I took it gratefully, still nervous about my shoes.

"Hi," I said.

"The car is here, and it's time to have some fun!"

The back seat of the car was long and roomy, but even so, I could feel the man's presence as if he was crammed in next to me. He had a certain something, a charisma, and I could feel a prickle of excitement for the night to come.

"You're not wearing a mask?" I said.

He grinned, tapping the breast pocket of his suit. "It's in here. I'm not going to put it on until we arrive - I'm afraid it reminds me of playing superheroes as a kid."

I laughed, taking him in. Somehow I couldn't imagine this suave, put-together man ever being a child, running around playing make-believe.

"Still," he continued, "rules of the party. All the guests are masked. And I suppose it is kind of a turn on when you're there. You're as sexy as hell in that feathered thing."

I was glad of the darkness in the car, as I was sure that I was blushing furiously. Had anyone ever told me that I was sexy before? I didn't think so. But the way he'd said it, so matter-of-fact, made me believe that it was true. I could feel my confidence rising.

"So, Mr Purple, tell me about this party."

"You don't have to call me that, really."

"What should I call you, then?"

He thought for a moment.

"Don't call me anything. Nobody at the party will. Sometimes you see people there who you recognise, but nobody uses names. Much like the Prism Club, really.

Except they give us the colour names so that they can figure out the...erm...logistics..."

He raised his eyebrows mockingly. I was starting to like him - he didn't take himself too seriously. Although I couldn't help but notice that he hadn't seemed that way when James had carried me down the stairs. I wanted to ask him more about James, but I sensed that mentioning him would be an instant mood-killer.

"As for the party - it's exactly what you think it will be. Lots of rich, beautiful people fucking each other's brains out. No small talk, no canapés, just sex. Does that bother you?"

At first I thought he was teasing me, but when I looked into his eyes I could see it was a genuine question - he wanted to know if I was comfortable with what would happen. I fumbled for my words, wanting to answer him as honestly as possible.

"I...I'm not bothered, that's not how I would describe it. I'm just...I don't know...inexperienced, I guess. Until I came to the club - I suppose you already realise this - I hadn't ever slept with anyone, and really I don't know enough about that side of me to know what I like and what I don't. I'm worried that once we're there, and things are happening, I won't like it."

He moved closer to me on the seat and took my hand gently.

"It's OK. I'm not going to make you do anything you don't want to do. You can tell me if it's too much. But tell me this - what's your absolute gut feeling?"

I met his gaze hesitantly.

"I'm excited. I think I'm going to like it."

The car swept onto the driveway of a large private house. Peering out of the window, I could see valets waiting to assist those who, unlike us, didn't have their own driver. Mr Purple slipped his mask on.

"What do you think?"

It was a plain black velvet, more like that of a highwayman than a superhero, in all honesty.

"I like it. It makes you look...dangerous."

His grin flashed white in the darkness.

"Maybe I am..."

The driver opened the door and he climbed out, turning to offer me his arm.

"You can ditch those bloody shoes, if you want."

I wanted to, I really did, but it seemed to wrong to be walking into a houseful of strangers completely barefoot.

"Maybe later," I said, gratefully accepting the assistance. I clung to him as we entered the mansion, more from nerves than reasons of balance. Beyond the door, a masked, bare-chested waiter was holding a silver tray filled with champagne flutes. Mr Purple took two, handing one to me.

"Bottoms up, as it were." He guided me through a set of large double doors.

Emboldened by the drink in my hand and the man on my arm, I took my first look around. And boy, was there a lot to see!

There were maybe twenty people in the room altogether, all masked, and all in various states of undress. A woman was lying on a purple chaise longue, completely naked, legs apart. There was a man with his head buried between her legs, licking her pussy, while a second was thrusting in and out of her mouth. Two more men stood over her, and she was pulling on their cocks. As I watched, one of the men groaned, shooting his cum over her breasts. She released him and he stepped back, and another took his place.

In a different corner, two women were writhing on the floor, engaged in licking each others pussies. They were being watched avidly by a couple who were fucking doggy-style.

Everywhere I looked, there were people screwing. I could feel a heat inside me at the thought that I could soon be one of them.

"Looks like we've arrived a little late - they seem to have started without us. How..." he paused, reached up and pushed my hair back off my face, "...rude."

My heart pounded in my chest as he touched me. Our eyes locked, and, as we stared, I felt his fingertip run slowly, ever so slowly, down my bare arm. It was more intimate than anything I had ever experienced, and I couldn't look away. I was hyper-aware of him, his closeness and his lithe, sensual body. His hand closed over mine, he smiled, and the spell was lifted slightly.

"We probably need to do something about these clothes. Are you ready for that?" he asked.

Strangely, I was. Although I was usually uncomfortable with being naked around strangers - who wouldn't be? - we were literally the only clothed people in the room, and it made us more conspicuous. I was aware of people glancing at us, and I wanted to blend in.

"Yes," I replied. "Do we put them somewhere?"

"There's a changing room. Come, I'll show you."

He led us back across the marbled tiles of the hall, to a pair of doors that looked like bathrooms - they were even labelled 'ladies' and 'gentlemen'. I felt a moment of panic when I realised he wouldn't be going in with me. I didn't yet feel relaxed enough to be left alone, and although I'd only known him for an evening, he was my only friend in this strange new world.

He caught the look in my eye.

"Go on, it will be OK. I'll be waiting right here for you."

He kissed me on the cheek, a light, reassuring kiss, and gently propelled me to the door marked 'ladies'.

Inside, I was surprised to find a room furnished much like a gym changing room. There were lockers, showers, and mirrors. The only real difference was the dim, sensuous lighting, and of course the artwork on the walls. It was moody, black and white photos that as far I could tell had been taken in this very house, and each one displayed beautiful, masked men and women in various sexual positions.

Anxious not to keep him waiting, I tore my gaze away and hurried over to one of the lockers. My first task was to rip off the hateful shoes and hurl them into the locker with all the contempt they deserved. But then, I wasn't sure how far to strip down. My outfit was a dress with a built in bra and a wisp of panties. I decided to store the dress, but leave the panties on for now. I still didn't quite have the nerve to walk around fully naked, and besides, I reasoned, if they got lost somewhere along the way, I could still get home with dignity as long as I had my dress.

That thought gave me pause for a second - it was the first time I'd thought of the Prism Club as being 'home'. I smiled to myself as I stripped down - maybe the experience was changing me after all.

Finally barefoot and topless, I knocked back the last of my champagne and abandoned the glass on a shelf with a few others. I took a deep breath, opened the door, and there he was, waiting for me.

Apart from his mask, he was completely naked. His body was good, lean and toned without being overly muscular. His cock hung down between his legs like a club. He seemed completely unabashed at being naked, and I felt some of my own awkwardness disappear.

He looked me up and down, a slow smile forming on his handsome face.

"You look perfect," he whispered, wrapping his arm around my waist.

The skin-on-skin contact was like electric heat, and I realised that I wanted him, very badly.

"What do you want to do first?" he murmured into my ear.

"Just...just us at first," I said.

"No problem."

He led me back into the first room, and over to a leather couch. I sat down, perched and unsure of how to begin. He sat next to me, and then slid a hand under my leg, pulling me so that I was lying on my back. The leather was cold on my skin, and it added to the sensations that were pulsating though me. He kissed me, roughly and passionately, and I felt my body respond. My back arched to meet him, and I pressed my breasts against his chest.

I could feel his cock growing hard against my thigh, and knowing that he wanted me, this handsome man, made the last of my inhibitions fall away. I was sexy, powerful, desirable, and I wanted him too. He slid down my body, caressing my breasts, gently biting the hard nipples in a way that made me cry out. I could see that some of the other people were starting to take notice, and I didn't care. I wanted them to watch, wanted them to see this sexy, handsome man taking me and fucking me right there in front of them.

His mouth descended lower, and I felt a sharp tug as he literally tore the wispy panties away, discarding them carelessly on the floor. I opened my thighs and his head was between my legs, tongue swirling around my clit as I gasped and moaned. And then he was back, suddenly face to face once more.

"I can't wait. I have to be inside you now," he muttered thickly into my ear. And with that, he thrust his cock inside me, kissing my neck feverishly. I moaned with pleasure - he was huge and perfect and the sensation of him inside me was exquisite. I was dimly aware of people creeping closer, watching him fuck me, but all I could really focus on was him, and what he was doing to me. I could feel an orgasm building up, and my hips started to buck.

"No, no." he growled into my ear. "Not yet, make yourself hold on. I want to watch you cumming."

This was agony! He was thrusting away and I wanted, needed to cum, but I somehow managed to hold it off. He groaned and I felt him cum inside me, then he withdrew. I was in a delirium of sexual arousal and frustration.

He pulled back, leaving me lying on the couch. I felt exposed, without him lying on top of me, as if I was fully naked for the first time. But it was good, freeing, delicious.

He traced the shape of my lips with his finger, and then spiralled down and down, over my breasts and belly, along my thigh. I twisted, trying to get his hand where I needed it the most, and he laughed.

"You really want this, don't you?" he said softly.

I nodded, unable to speak.

"They all want you to have it, too," he said, indicating around him. A small crowd of naked men and women were now standing around the couch, watching my naked body avidly. I didn't care. I didn't care about anything in the whole world apart from the ache between my thighs. I moved again, trying to rub my pussy against his hand.

"I guess I'd better let you have what you want, then..."

He started to rub my clit, and I gasped with pleasure. As he expertly worked me, a hand came down from the crowd and started to play with my breast, pulling and pinching at the erect nipple. Someone else - a woman - knelt by the couch and started to kiss the other breast, flicking her tongue in a way that sent electricity straight down to my clit. I could feel the orgasm building again, and I thought to myself that he if he denied me again, I would simply explode. But he didn't. He looked deep into my eyes and nodded, rubbing me harder and harder, faster and faster. I let out a scream as my climax hit, writhing and bucking on the couch as the hands caressing me tried to keep up. Fireworks exploded in my mind, and time stood still as the waves washed over me. Finally, it ended, leaving me drifting back to consciousness.

I looked up at the crowd surrounding me. All the men were hard, and I felt a thrill of power. I had done that! They were hard because they looked at me, saw me as vulnerable and exposed as can be - naked and cumming - and they liked it.

He leaned over and kissed me softly. I could taste myself on his lips.

"Did you like that?" he asked.

"Yes," I said. "I want more."

He grinned.

"So do I, sweetheart. So do I. But don't worry, we've barely even started. Let's get a drink and explore a little."

"But what about them?" I whispered.

"They'll still be here when we get back."

He took me by the hand and I got up from the couch. The crowd started to back away, reluctantly, looking for new entertainment. I saw a man pick up my torn panties and wrap them round his cock, using them to jerk himself off. I had never felt so sexy, so desired in all my life.

"The key to life," he said quietly, as he escorted me away, "is to never give people what they want right away. The longer they want it, the sweeter it is..."

He had a point, I realised. He made me wait, and I'd liked it more. No doubt, those people that had watched me would feel the same. We headed up the staircase, and though into another room. This one was done up in the style of a dungeon - in fact, it reminded me of the room where I'd lost my virginity just a few days ago. He seemed to be aware of the connection.

"Familiar, huh?"

"It seems like everyone has a dungeon." I said, laughing.

"Ah, this one is different, though," he said.

"Why?"

"Because in this one, you get to wield the whip..."

He sauntered over to a couple. The woman was bent over a bench, the man towering over her, holding a whip with strands of leather dangling from it.

"Do you mind if my friend has a try? She's only ever been on the receiving end."

"Be my guest," the stranger said, handing me the whip. Both men stood back, ready to enjoy the show.

"Do you...is it OK?" I asked the woman. She was face-down, so it was impossible to know how she felt about it.

"She's OK with it," the man answered for her. He seemed amused by my politeness.

I looked at the curve of her bottom. It was slightly pink, as if she'd taken a few lashes already. Tentatively, I brought the whip down.

"Harder!" said the man. I looked at him questioningly. "She won't even feel that, my love. Give her what she wants!"

My eyes met Mr Purple's, and he nodded slightly. I knew what that meant - give her what she wants, but take my time about it.

I began to lightly swat at her backside, each time increasing the pressure slightly. Soon there was an audible smack every time I brought the whip down. The woman was moaning with pleasure, her cheeks turning redder and redder. Finally I was beating her, bringing down the whip with all my strength, and she started to beg.

"Please, finish me, please!"

Instinctively I knew what to do. I grabbed her arm and flipped her over, so that she was lying on her back. I brushed the tendrils of the whip down over her body, and watched her moan and quiver. Then, just like he had done to me downstairs, I slid my hand between her legs. She was soaking wet. I started to stroke her clit, occasionally sliding a finger in and out of her tight pussy. It was strange, touching another woman like that - it was just like touching myself but at the same time totally different.

I could feel her pussy starting to spasm, and I knew she was close to cumming. With my other hand, I raised the whip once more, and began to lightly flog her breasts, first one, then the other, taking care not to go too hard on the delicate flesh, whilst all the time rhythmically massaging her clit. She screamed with pleasure, her juices gushing out onto my hand, and I laid down my whip, thrilled with myself.

"Good job," her partner said. "You're a natural at that."

"What now?" I asked, as we walked away.

"There's a room along here that's...well, basically a free-for-all. Would you enjoy that, do you think?"

"Sounds good." I tucked my arm in his as he led me down the corridor. I could hear the sounds of men and women being fucked as we approached, and it was like music to my ears...

This room was an actual bedroom, but with a twist. There were three huge beds, each one big enough for six people to sleep comfortably. Not that anyone here was sleeping. Two of the beds were fully occupied, but on the third one lay a man and a woman. They were naked and masked, like everyone else, but they were whispering to each other and looking around.

"First-timers," came the murmur in my ear. "You fancy it?"

"Sure," I said.

We went over to the bed, and the couple smiled up at us, moving over to make room. I lay on the bed next to the other woman, and she tentatively lay a hand on my arm. I felt a sudden rush of empowerment and desire - she was more nervous, less confident than me, and it seemed to transform me into a bold, strong woman. I kissed her, deeply and passionately, and I knew the men enjoyed watching it.

Mr Purple lay down next to me, and began to stroke my back. As the kiss broke off, he reached over and pushed her head down until it was between my legs. I felt myself instantly get wet as she began to lick me, long, slow strokes that gave me shivers all over. He was kissing me now, occasionally breaking away to watch her working away at my pussy. The other man knelt over us, cock in hand, stroking it as he watched his wife lick me out.

She was good, and again I could feel the orgasm building. Suddenly I wanted it stronger, faster, and I writhed about, grabbing hold of her hair and pressing my pussy onto her face. The men were squeezing my tits, hard and firmly, and Mr Purple was still kissing me as I started to cum, my cries muffled in his mouth. But I still wasn't satisfied. I needed to be filled - filled by a cock.

The woman sat up, face shiny and sticky with my pussy juice.

"Now him," her husband said, nodding at Mr Purple.

She bent her head once more, and began to suck his cock. The husband, meanwhile, pulled me into a kneeling position on the bed, and got behind me. I was facing Mr Purple, so that I could watch him as the husband fucked me from behind. It was amazing to watch him, the desire and ecstasy flickering over his masked face as the woman deep throated him. Then the man entered me, filling me up and giving me the satisfaction that I craved.

Mr Purple leaned forward, over the woman's bobbing head, and began to kiss me once more, and although there was two other people there, it felt like we were the only two that mattered – all the rest were just fuck-toys, here for our pleasure and enjoyment. As the complete stranger rammed his cock into me, I felt yet another climax coming, and I gave in to the rush of feelings, moaning and screaming as he jack-hammered away. I saw Mr Purple's face contort as he shot his load down the woman's throat, and then it was her husband's turn. He groaned as he filled me with his hot, thick spunk.

"Thank you," he said, climbing down off the bed. And with that, he took his wife's hand and they wandered off, no doubt in search of new pleasures.

Mr Purple snuggled up next to me.

"You really liked this, didn't you?"

"Yes," I admitted. "I'm surprised that I enjoyed it so much."

"Good. So have I. But now, we best get back to the club, before one of us turns into a pumpkin..."

Mr Purple had walked me to my door, kissed my cheek, and left, promising to be in touch after I had finished the Prism Club. I was touched by that - I felt like I had made a friend. And speaking of friends...

"How was it?" she asked, as I opened my bedroom door.

Davina was sitting on the sofa.

"It was actually really, really good fun," I said. "Come into the bathroom while I have a bath, and I'll tell you all about it."

"Well, someone's getting more comfortable with themselves!" she said, smiling. "And what happened to your knickers? Did you go out without them?"

"Last seen wrapped round the cock of a lovely gentleman whom I later discovered to be a Member of Parliament," I giggled.

I lay in the bath and gossiped with Davina, telling her all about my evening, the charming Mr Purple, and the people I had met at the party.

"What's next, Davina?" I asked. "Didn't you say something about exhibitionism?"

"Ah, yes," she replied. "Mr Yellow, the pop-star creator. Well, to be honest, it's a bit more than just exhibitionism, but I wanted to wait until after tonight to tell you, so that you didn't freak out."

"Okay..." I said, "what is it?"

"Well, you'll be called Saffron."

I liked that. "Don't they say saffron is more expensive than gold, gram for gram?"

"Yes, they do," she said, smiling wryly, "And it's funny that you've brought up money. Mr Yellow likes prostitutes."

"So, I'll have to sleep with prostitutes?"

"No, Saffron," she said kindly, "You'll have to become one..."

SAFFRON

It was three days after my sex club adventure, and I was bored. After the first Prism Club experience, I had needed the time to recover, but now I was finding that wasn't really the case any more. I was actually looking forward to my next adventure - something that surprised me. The old me - nervous, timid, shy was changing, and I was becoming something else. But what that was, I still didn't know.

One thing that hadn't changed was my shock at living as if I was a wealthy woman. Although none of it was mine, I had seemingly everything at my disposal. My 'room' was larger and better appointed than my entire flat. And the things, the lovely girlie things - I had no idea that I enjoyed it so much, mostly because I'd never had luxuries before. In my wardrobe was a seemingly unlimited supply of beautiful designer clothes.

I'd always thought that designer stuff was a rip-off - you just paid more for the famous name that was usually emblazoned all over the clothes. But now, being able to get up close and experience the clothes, I realised that they were in a different league. They were quality fabrics, cut to drape and flatter. And wearing them changed me, too. Because I looked better, I felt more confident, which means I held myself better. I no longer had the desire to shrink into the wall - I wanted people to notice me.

I was also enjoying all the make-up, lotions and potions that I found in the bathroom. Davina was teaching me how to use them to best effect.

"Less is more", she seemed to say a million times a day. I could see that she had a point, though. Make-up wasn't for disguising your natural features, it was for highlighting them in a flattering way. For the first time ever in my life, I was looking in the mirror and seeing my good points, instead of just a collection of flaws and imperfections that needed hiding from the world.

Even my views on food were changing. The Prism Club provided all my meals, and they were always luxurious dishes. I'd worried initially that I would put weight on, but I was finding that wasn't the case - if anything, I was losing some of the flab around my belly. I mentioned this to Davina, and she pointed out that by eating good quality food, I wasn't binging on sweets and junk food, looking for a sugar hit to get me through the day.

All in all, I was enjoying my new, rich-person lifestyle, and the thought of going back to my old life - the grubby flat, the penny-pinching, the failed job hunting - filled me with terror. I was more determined than ever to complete the programme and accept the Club's help to become a successful woman, standing on my own two feet. So I was pleased when Davina announced that my next assignment would begin tomorrow.

"This one's different, though," she said.

"Different how?" I asked.

"It's more involved, more work. You'll spend much less time with the member. And it won't be here, at the club."

"Where will it be at?"

"Well, he likes prostitutes. So that's what you'll be for him. You'll see clients, take the money - which you get to keep -and he'll...watch. Secretly. Obviously none of that could happen here at the club."

"So, what? I'm going to stand on a street corner?"

She smiled. "How much do you actually know about prostitution?"

"Honestly, not a lot. I've seen the crack whores at Kings Cross station, and apart from that all I know is what I've seen on TV - drug addicts who mostly seem to get murdered."

I was feeling less confident about this by the minute. I didn't mind the sex, but danger was another thing.

Davina placed a soft hand on my shoulder. "Relax. Yes, there are prostitutes who take drugs and stand on street corners and sometimes get murdered. But they're not the only kind of working girl."

She sat down and adopted a 'giving a lecture to the clueless new girl' pose. It was one I was rapidly becoming familiar with.

"At the top of the tree, there's high class escorts. Model types, get paid thousands of pounds to party with, and of course fuck, the lucky few who can afford their services. Private jets, Mediterranean island villas, class A narcotics and champagne all the way."

She raised an eyebrow at the bloom of optimism in my eyes.

"You won't be one of those. Well, not unless you want to when you leave. His deal is watching, and the kind of security those guys have doesn't allow for voyeurs."

Ah well. It would be an interesting career option to consider, though. Davina continued.

"A little further down, you have your standard escorts. Either agency-run or independent. They advertise on the internet as 'companionship only', but that's just a front. They generally charge one or two hundred pounds an hour, and at that price range they tend to attract the average joe who'd saved up to treat himself. The appointment is either outcall - you go to them, or incall - they come to you."

That didn't sound too bad. It wasn't champagne and jets, but the idea of getting paid two hundred quid an hour was still mind blowing. I'd never worked for anything more than minimum wage.

"Is that part of the job? Or just another slide in your PowerPoint presentation of prostitution?" I teased.

She rolled her eyes. "Is it my fault that you're so woefully naive? Yes, it will likely come up, although he changes his mind about what he wants from day to day. Obviously incall only - there's a flat that's equipped with viewing facilities and you'd work out of there."

I nodded. "What else is there?"

"Then, there's the parlours, which are pretty much one up from the street. The all-night seedy massage parlours. The way it works there is different. The parlour advertises the services, men just turn up without an appointment and pick a girl -there'll be a choice of three or so. She takes him into a 'massage room', does the deed, and he pays her. She gives a percentage of that to the parlour and keeps the rest."

"Is that so bad?"

"Well, the money's crap. You might charge sixty quid to fuck a guy, and then turn half of that over to the house. It's tiring - you might see ten clients in a night. And the people there are..."

She wrinkled her nose.

"I don't mean to be snobby, really I don't, god knows neither one of us was born with a silver spoon in our mouths, but they're a pretty rough crowd. Like I say, it's only one up from the streets."

"And does our voyeur billionaire like the parlours?" I asked.

"Yes, he certainly does. There's a couple that have an arrangement with him, where he can watch. They've no idea who he is, of course, the viewing room is accessed separately to the main building."

"So, you've told me about the business, what about him? What does he get from it? He's the one I need to please, not the customers."

"Honestly? He thinks it's degrading, and that's what he gets off on. That's why he likes the parlours so much - watching a girl take on guy after guy for pocket change."

Her expression changed, and she looked away.

"After you've finished your shift, he'll bring you back here in the car. He expects you to give him the come-on, touting for business as it were, and he likes it if you've not showered since the last one. If you do that, he'll be happy."

"OK, I'll do that." I said.

She got up from the chair. "Get some rest, I'll see you later. I need to sort your outfits out."

She seemed odd, kind of distant, but she was gone before I could ask her about it. So instead I took her advice and drew a foamy bath, wondering all the while what tomorrow would bring. Davina still hadn't returned by the time I went to sleep.

When I awoke, a small pile of clothes were waiting for me, folded neatly on the chair. Clearly, Davina had sneaked in as I was sleeping. I couldn't help but feel that she was being evasive with me, and I had a horrible suspicion that her reticence was related to my latest assignment. But why? Was it this new billionaire, Mr Yellow? I knew he wasn't the one that she'd fallen for, the one that had caused her to leave the programme. That one had left the club entirely.

Maybe it was just my imagination. Maybe she was busy, or had other things on her mind. I had to remember that, although Davina was really my only contact, she probably had an entire life outside of her work. There was a note on top of the pile of clothes.

Spoke to Mr Yellow last night – you need to be ready to leave by lunchtime. Wear these clothes, and do your own hair and make-up. You'll be back by midnight. Remember why you're doing this!
D.

Well, that was... unusual. I'd never been allowed to do my own beauty preparations before. Maybe Davina was ill? I examined the clothes that she had left for me, and suddenly things started to get a little clearer...

The clothes were – there was no other way to describe them – cheap and tacky. I was hardly a fashion snob, I'd been dressing myself on a severely limited budget my entire life, but this stuff was awful. A bright yellow skirt that barely covered my backside, and was made out of some sort of shiny, stretchy fabric. The top was a black scratchy, nylon lace thing – long-sleeved but completely see-through. A pair of black patent stilettos finished off the look. At first, I thought the shoes were second-hand – they were scuffed and the heels were worn, but on further examination I realised that they were new shoes, made to look old. There was underwear, too. It was made of the same scratchy material as the top. The bra had holes over the nipples, and the knickers were crotchless.

Great. Clearly, I wasn't going to be one of the high

end prostitutes, then. And this was why I was being allowed to do my own hair and make-up – my skills with a brush were obviously the cosmetic equivalent of this... this outfit. I glanced at the note again. Remember why you're doing this! Really? Was Davina that fashion conscious that she couldn't bring herself to put together this look for me? It wouldn't surprise me, I thought to myself, amused. I checked the time – there was still a few hours before I had to go. I decided to take yet another long, luxurious bath. I might have to dress like a cheap whore, but at least I could smell like a lady!

I stayed in the bath until the water turned cold, forcing me out. I put on the horrible outfit, and checked my reflection. I was shocked. Although I did look exactly as I had expected – a prostitute, and the clothes looked as cheap as they promised, somehow the whole look was not exactly 'streetwalker', more like 'Hollywood does streetwalker'. My body looked good – long and lean and toned. And I knew for a fact that it was nothing of the sort. I put the heels on and wobbled up and down. The thick carpet wasn't the easiest surface to walk on, but on the marble bathroom floor I found I wasn't actually that bad. I could feel the first glimmer of confidence, despite the fact that my bum was practically hanging out.

As directed, I did my own make up. I didn't try anything fancy, just the usual slap that I would do for a night out. Even that looked better – the products here at the club were more expensive than my own humble kit, and it showed on my less-than-perfectly made up face. I tried to imagine what the day would be like. I was guessing that I would be in one of the massage parlours that Mr Yellow enjoyed. It would be strange, interacting with people who didn't know about the club, about me. They would think that I was just another down-on-my-luck woman. And it wasn't just the people who worked at the massage parlour – I would have to talk to clients, too. That would be different to the people I had met at the swingers club. There, we had all been equals, each one of those attending for the same thing. I knew the dynamic of power would be different in a massage parlour, but I didn't know how. Who was in charge? The prostitute, because the clients wanted to sleep with her, or the client, because the customer was always right?

It was unnerving to think that I would be alone for most of this task, at least as far as the club was concerned. Mr Red and Mr Purple had been by my side the entire time, but it sounded like I'd barely see Mr Yellow until the end. At least he'd be able to see me though, so I would be safer than it first appeared. I was surprised to find that I was much more nervous than I'd been prior to the other two assignments. I think it was the unknown element of it all.

A knock on the door snapped me out of my reverie. I knew it wasn't Davina – she'd have simply opened the door and entered. I hobbled over on the thick carpet and opened up. It was the chauffeur, the one who had brought me here on my very first time. I realised I didn't know his name, but I didn't want to ask. I felt uncomfortable – he was wearing full livery and an outdoor coat, and I wasn't wearing very much of anything at all.

"Are you ready to leave, Miss Saffron?" he asked politely, to his credit looking me in the eye and nowhere else.

"Yes, of course," I said. I followed him down the now-familiar corridor. When we got to the staircase, a face flashed into my mind – James. He had carried me down the stairs because I was struggling in my heels. I was managing much better today, and I almost wished he was there to see it. Not completely, though. It was stupid – he worked at the club, and he knew about the pseudonyms, so he certainly knew why I was there and what I was doing. So why would I be so embarrassed, for him to see me in this tacky whore's outfit? I tried to push him out of my mind. I didn't want to develop a crush on him. In a place like this, it would be insanity. I made an effort to pull my thoughts back to the here and now.

When the chauffeur opened the front doors, I was surprised. Instead of the gleaming Bentley, there was a clapped-out old minicab in its place. It made sense, I suppose – if I was being dropped off at a massage parlour, I would need to blend in. I could see there was a man already sitting in the back of the cab. The chauffeur opened the door, and I tried to climb in with as much dignity as possible. Sadly, that wasn't very much. The step up was high, and I had to lean forward and grab one of the seats to haul myself in. Between the miniskirt and the crotchless knickers, I was well aware that I was giving the chauffeur an absolute eyeful. Thankfully, there were no passers-by.

I flopped down onto one of the seats, opposite the passenger. He had clearly enjoyed watching my entrance. He was smirking, looking my body up and down, and winking at the chauffeur. He was older than the other two had been, and to be honest, much less attractive. I had known from the start that I couldn't possibly be expected to fancy all seven billionaires, but this one was the first disappointment. He had a sleazy mannerism about him. It was hard to pinpoint exactly why, but I instinctively didn't like him. I remembered that he was the record company owner, and I wondered how many hopeful young starlets had been on the receiving end of that lecherous grin.

"Well, sweetheart," he said. "Don't you look the part? I think you'll take to this like, well, like a whore to cock..."

I felt myself begin to blush, and fought the urge to look away and show my embarrassment. After all, I didn't care what he thought of me, did I? And yes, what I was doing wasn't exactly the most morally virtuous thing on earth, but neither was what he was doing, either. I looked him in the eye.

"Thank you, you're very kind. I'm sure we'll have a lovely day," I said smoothly, channelling my inner Davina. He looked disappointed, and I remembered that what did it for him was the humiliation. Shit! As much as I wanted to show this sleazebag that he didn't intimidate me, I also needed to make him happy. I shifted about in my seat, trying to tug the miniskirt a little lower, as if trying to cover myself. His eyes lit up.

"You leave that alone, sweetheart. Here." He leaned forward in his seat, and grasped my knees with both hands, pushing my legs apart. My recoil was entirely involuntary. He leaned back.

"You just sit like that, that's perfect. Just sit there and keep quiet, and we'll be there in no time."

He was sitting opposite me. My open legs, and the crotchless knickers I was wearing meant that he was staring directly at my exposed pussy. He was grinning, idly rubbing his cock through his trousers. My humiliation was no longer faked – it was all too real. Sitting there, in the back of the cab, being forbidden to speak or move while this arsehole stared at me was simply awful. I knew that my entire face was bright red, but I was too busy trying to hold back the tears. He would never get those, I swore to myself fiercely.

We weren't 'there in no time', either. The journey seemed to take forever. Leafy Belgravia was far behind us – we were in one of the roughest areas of London before the cab finally stopped. It was a notoriously dangerous place, and I'd never visited it before. Still staring at my crotch, he spoke.

"Out you get, sweetheart."

He nodded at the building we had pulled up in front of. It was a rundown kebab house, and it was closed. Metal shutters were pulled down over the door and windows, and they were covered in graffiti. Was this a joke? Then I noticed the second door, leading up presumably to the flat above the shop. A sign in the flat window said 'Passions Massage'. It didn't look like a massage parlour – it looked exactly like what it was, a brothel. Suddenly, my new fear was not the staff or the clients, or even this lecherous old man, it was a police raid. I hoped to God that the Prism Club had the police in their back pockets.

I climbed out of the cab, hideously aware that I was flashing Mr Yellow the same view that the poor chauffeur had received previously. Except no doubt Mr Yellow was getting off on it. I don't know what it was exactly that made my skin crawl – whether it was the humiliation, or the man himself. But either way, I knew that this one was going to be a challenge.

Without looking back, I made my way over to the Passions Massage front door. It looked neglected and rundown. The paint was peeling in places, and the brass was pitted and flaking. But the intercom and camera looked brand-new and state-of-the-art. Clearly, there was more to this picture than met the eye. I wondered if all brothels had this kind of security, or if this was a result of their association with the Prism Club. Hopefully, I would never find out. Once I had finished the programme, I would be a wealthy woman. And hey, I thought to myself, if it doesn't work out, at least I have a trade to fall back on now. I pressed the intercom button, and the door buzzed loudly, clicking as the lock was released. Nobody spoke to me, though. Apprehensive now, I pushed open the battered front door and went inside.

The door opened directly onto a narrow staircase. It was dingy and rundown, the frayed carpet an indeterminate brown colour. It seemed like the only way was up, so that's exactly what I did, praying all the way that I wouldn't meet a client coming out. I wouldn't know what to say! Should I respect their privacy and ignore them, or practice good customer service and be friendly, or even sexy? It was strange – despite the completely unusual situation, I felt the same way I did every time I started a new job. Like I didn't know what I was doing, and I was about to be sacked. I couldn't get sacked from this job, though. I was sure that failure to complete the shift would mean removal from the Prism Club programme. No matter what, I had to succeed.

There was a second door at the top of the stairs. This one had no intercom, but I was clearly being watched, as the lock clicked open automatically for me. I took a deep breath, trying to hide my nerves, and pushed it open. It seemed to be a reception area. There was a high desk, with a woman perched on a stool behind it. There were some couches forming a lounge area and facing a small TV that was showing a porn film. Thankfully, there was no one else there.

"You Saffron?" the woman behind the counter barked. Her tone was harsh and unfriendly – this was no Davina, here to guide me and support me.

"Yes," I said. I felt as if I should say more, but I was lost for words. Whomever she was, this woman did not seem very happy about me being there.

She looked me up and down, disdainfully. "You ever worked the parlours before?"

There was no point in lying. "No," I said.

She sighed, as if overwhelmed by the burden of this news. Lighting a cigarette, she shuffled around the counter towards me.

"Meeting area," she said, gesturing towards the

couches. "The punters sit there, and whatever girls are free do a line-up. He picks the one he wants. If he picks you, you're working out of room three."

She crossed the meeting area and headed off down a small dark corridor. I trailed behind her, inhaling her cigarette smoke and wanting to cough, but not quite daring to. She struck me as somebody who would take offence at the slightest provocation, and then beat the crap out of the offender. She reminded me of some of the nastier girls at school. We passed other doors on our way down the corridor, and I could hear the sounds of sex coming from all of them. The horrible woman flung open the end door. Of course it's the end one, I thought. Mr Yellow will be on the other side of the wall in the property next door, cock in hand. I hoped he didn't notice that I was afraid of the receptionist. Maybe he didn't watch unless there was action.

The room was tacky, but surprisingly clean, compared to the rest of the place. It was all leopard print wallpaper and hot pink fabric, with the most dominant feature of the room being a large bed. It was an ordinary bed, not a massage table. It seemed that beyond the name, Passions Massage didn't bother to hide what they did.

"Condoms in there," she said, pointing to a bedside table. "You always use a condom. I don't give a fuck what you do out on the street corner, but you won't be spreading your diseases in here, lady."

I was ninety percent outraged that she thought I had sexually transmitted diseases, and ten percent relieved. If she thought I'd worked the streets, then I must be fitting in better than I realised. I pushed the thought out of my mind, though. Yes, I was in a situation where being mistaken for a common prostitute was a good thing, but I really didn't need a moment of clarity right now. What I needed was to get through this day.

"I always use a condom," I said firmly, even though that wasn't actually true. I'd only had sex with the two billionaires, and people at the swingers party, and condoms had never come up. Everybody involved had had full screening for disease. I wasn't even sure if I knew how to put a condom on a man. I wasn't about to tell her that, though.

She snorted disbelievingly. "Prices. It costs them thirty quid to walk through the door. That buys them a half-hour massage. If that's what they ask for, they're Old Bill. You massage them for five minutes, excuse yourself, and come and find me. You understand?"

"I understand," I said. "Do Old Bill come in a lot?" I felt self-conscious about using the phrase 'Old Bill' instead of police, like I was trying too hard to be like her, so that she would like me.

"Nah," she said. "Not on official business, anyway. If they shut down all the brothels, where would they go to get their cocks sucked? Speaking of, a blowjob is twenty quid. For an extra five, they can finish in your mouth. For an extra ten, you'll swallow it." It didn't seem optional. "Full sex is forty, and you throw the oral in for free. Anal is twenty on top. You don't charge anything other than those prices. It causes trouble. Girls start undercutting each other, leads to fights."

Undercutting each other? Jesus Christ! I was already shocked at how little I would be charging to have full, intimate sex with a complete stranger. I nodded my assent.

"So a punter comes in, wants the works. How much do you charge him?" Her eyes were like gimlets. Clearly, this was the only part that mattered to her.

"Ninety quid," I said confidently. She seemed pleased. Evidently, some of her girls weren't so good at adding up.

"That's right. You get the money up front. First thirty

goes to the house, then it's a 50-50 split. Standard appointment is half an hour. If he wants double, he pays double. We don't piss about with discounts. Once you're done, clean yourself up." She nodded at a curtain in the corner. "Sink and shitter through there. You have five minutes to get clean and dressed, and back out into the meeting area. Any questions?"

"How busy will it be?" I was working a six-hour shift. Potentially, that was ten or eleven clients, with the crappy break times factored in. That was a hell of a lot of men for anyone, let alone me. I hoped they didn't all want anal. And even if they did, I'd only be coming out with 300 pounds or so. Although that seemed like a great deal of money, I didn't know if I could physically take it.

"Well, you're not on the busiest shift. You're a fresh face, though, and that will count for something. You might see five or six punters."

That didn't seem as bad. Although if I only had five, and they only wanted basic blowjobs, I'd be walking out of here with 50 pounds. That made me feel strange. If I was going to do this, I wanted it to be worth my while. This thinking was ridiculous, though. At the club, I didn't need money. The finest of everything was provided for me. And after the club, I'd be a wealthy woman. Caring about this was completely redundant, and yet I did. I think that perhaps, deep down, part of me didn't believe that I would ever be rich and successful. I was expecting to fail, eventually, and if I did… well, my Passions Massage money would be all I had. Another thought occurred to me.

"How many girls are there? Besides me?"

"Worried about the competition?" Her expression was mocking. "Two others. Both old Toms. Can't get the young ones to do any of the shifts earlier than midnight."

A bleeping noise sounded, down the corridor.

"Look lively, girl," she said. "The other two are busy,

so this one is yours." She turned and stalked back to her reception desk, and I followed anxiously.

"Sit," she hissed at me, peering at the security camera monitor. I couldn't see the screen. I suppose it didn't matter, really. Whoever he was, he would be my first client. Punter, I corrected myself. They call them punters. The door at the top of the stairs opened, and a man walked through.

My heart sank. I hadn't been expecting much, but even so... He looked like something off the sex offenders register. Creepy and weird. The witch beamed at him.

"Geoffrey! How are you, me old mucker?"

"All the better for seeing you, Destiny," he said to her cleavage. I smirked internally at her choice of name.

"We got a new girl for you," she said. "Saffron." There was a tiny edge to her voice when she said the word Saffron, and I knew that she had detected my amusement at the name Destiny. I hoped to God that her fawning over Geoffrey meant that she wouldn't beat the shit out of me, at least not until he'd gone. Geoffrey turned to look at me.

"You're a tasty one," he said to me, licking his lips. "Is she extra?" he asked the woman. I raised an eyebrow. For all her insistence that the girls stick to the price list, it was obvious that Destiny herself wasn't above bunging a little extra on the bill.

"Not to you, Geoffrey my love," she said. "Saffron darling, take Geoffrey through and look after him. He's one of the special ones!"

"Follow me," I squeaked. I couldn't bring myself to take his arm. I walked into room three and just stood there. I didn't know what to do, but I figured that Special Geoffrey was a regular. He fished in his wallet, and produced a crumpled pile of notes. They were slightly damp, as if he'd been clutching them in his sweaty palm.

I checked the money – fifty pounds.

"A blow job?" I said.

"That's right," he said. "She said you were regular price, for me."

"I know," I said mindlessly. I felt completely frozen, and I didn't know how to begin. What was expected of me? Should I just drop to my knees and suck him off, or was there supposed to be a seduction? Luckily, Geoffrey knew the drill. He unzipped his trousers, pulled out a small, pale cock, and sat on the end of the bed.

I walked over to him, slowly. Not to be seductive – it was simply because taking that man's dick in my mouth was the last thing I wanted. I wasn't intimidated by him, if anything, I actually felt sorry for him. But he would be the first person that I ever had sexual contact with, and didn't feel attracted to. I knelt down in front of him, and then I remembered...

I remembered the real reason why I was there. I'd become so caught up in learning the brothel process, and dealing with the tenacious Destiny, that somehow it had slipped my mind. Mr Yellow was watching me, spying on me. He was going to watch me through the wall, watch me degrade myself by sucking this sad little man's cock, and he was going to get off on it. I suddenly felt terrible, shamed and humiliated. I felt my face flush red and hated myself for it, not wanting to give Mr Yellow the satisfaction of seeing it. Geoffrey, on the other hand, was oblivious.

"Not yet! I've got half an hour. Don't you be trying to get me out early, I know all your tricks!"

"Well what, then?" I snapped. I was sick of this already. I didn't know what to do, how to act, and I knew that it was all part of the attraction for the sleazy billionaire on the other side of the wall. Geoffrey looked taken aback – obviously the other girls were much nicer to him. I suppose they had to be, but I didn't. Yes you do, I reminded myself. What other option do you have? It was true. If I walked out of here right now, I wouldn't even have Geoffrey's – I did the maths – ten sodding pounds. If I stayed for the whole shift, bitching at the punters, it wouldn't be humiliating enough for Mr Yellow, and I'd be out of the programme.

I plastered an ingratiating smile on my face, and placed a hand on Geoffrey's knee. "What you want me to do? I'm all yours…"

He perked up. "Get your tits out, and let me have a play with them. Stand up, stand up."

I realised that standing, Mr Yellow would have an even better view. There was nothing else to be done, I had to play to my audience. I would pretend to be humiliated, get this awful day over and done with, and never look back. I'd never have to see any of these people again, not even the billionaire. I didn't want to be a singer, the only thing I needed from him was approval to move onto the next stage. These were the thoughts that ran through my head as I got to my feet.

Geoffrey pawed at me eagerly, not waiting for me to undress. He pushed the lace top up to my neck, grabbing at my boobs in their peephole bra.

"Oh, you've got cracking tits," he said, kneading them like bread. He leaned forward, tongue sticking out, and began to lick my nipple where it protruded from the cheap lace. "You like that, don't you? Oh yes you do, you dirty girl."

With Geoffrey focused on my boobs, I was able to compose my face into a mask of shame, for the benefit of Mr Yellow. But Geoffrey wasn't done.

"That's making you wet, isn't it? I bet you've got a tight wet juicy pussy now. Let's have a look, then." He was pulling my hips, turning me around like I was an inanimate object. "Bend over, girl, let your pal Geoffrey see that pussy."

Mechanically, I bent over. I hadn't expected this. From the way Destiny had ran through the pricelist, I had thought that a blow job would be just that – a blow job. Not being mauled like a piece of meat. My feigned humiliation was becoming all too genuine. Bent over, I could feel that the miniskirt had come right up, and Geoffrey could see everything through the crotchless knickers. I could feel his hot breath on my thighs.

"That's it, girl," he said. "Look at those knickers, you're a right little slut, aren't you?" He started to rub my pussy, poking his fingers deep inside me. "You're quiet, though." Again, he seemed disappointed, and I realised what he wanted. Dutifully, I began to moan as he prodded me ineptly.

"Oh yeah, you're loving this, you dirty bitch. Do want me to fuck you? Do you want me to stick my dick in your tight little snatch?"

No, I fucking well did not. "It's an extra twenty quid," I said breathily.

The finger-stabbing increased. "You don't mean that, girl," he said. "Way I see it, you're fucking gagging for it. If I fuck you in your tight little box, it's a treat for both of us. If you just suck me off, I'm leaving you frustrated, and old Geoffrey is too much of a gentleman to do that."

"Twenty. Quid." My tone was completely flat, devoid of all the passion I had been faking. In that moment, I didn't care about the club, about my goals, about the endgame. I just knew that I'd rather walk away with nothing then fuck this loser for free. The fingers withdrew, and I turned round quickly.

"I ain't got another twenty quid," he said sulkily. "I've been saving up for this. We're not all like you, making hundreds of pounds an hour selling your dirty pussy to anybody that wants. You fucking slag. You'll just have to suck me off and have done with it."

I got back on my knees, ashamed once more. The

moment of giddy liberation had passed, and I knew that I had to please Geoffrey, even though all I wanted to do was punch him in the face. I knew that Mr Yellow would have enjoyed Geoffrey's tirade, too.

The small, white cock was fully erect, and Geoffrey grabbed my hair, forcing my head down roughly onto it. Despite my distaste, I wanted this over. From what he'd said, he would leave after he had cum, even if his time wasn't up. I began to suck him as hard as I could, running my lips up and down his meagre length, swirling my tongue over the head of his cock. He kept his grip on my hair, holding my head in place and pushing me down.

"Oh yes, girl, that's it! Suck my cock, you dirty whore. You love it, you all love it…"

I could feel his cock starting to twitch inside my mouth. He was going to cum at any moment. I tried to push back and slide him out of my mouth, but I couldn't. His grip on my hair was like iron. He groaned, and waves of acrid spunk flooded my mouth.

"That's it, bitch, take it all. Swallow it down, I'll pay you, I swear!"

I didn't exactly have a choice – he still had his cock in my mouth and the cum was choking me. Reluctantly, I swallowed his load, and he finally let go of my head. I leapt to my feet.

"That's an extra tenner," I said.

He stood up, tucking his cock away fussily.

"I already told you, I ain't got no more money," he said, smugly. "I'll pay you extra next time."

It was too much. The sleazy, horrible place, the unseen presence of Mr Yellow, and now Geoffrey's self-satisfied smile and talk of next time. The taste of his spunk still filled my mouth, and I felt my stomach roil. I lurched for the curtain, ripping it aside to find an old toilet. I hung over the bowl, puking my guts up. My shame was complete.

When I had finally stopped throwing up, and rinsed my mouth out with water from the sink, Geoffrey had left the room. I picked up the sweaty notes – he obviously knew better than to rip the house off – and made my way back to the reception area. Destiny was behind the counter, and there were two older women sitting on the couches, drinking tea -the prostitutes. The other prostitutes, a voice in my mind piped up. I had accepted money to suck a man's cock, which made me just the same.

"How much did he do you for?" Destiny said, holding out a hand for her share of the cash.

"What do you mean?" I asked.

"He always tries to rip the new girls off," one of the older women said, "and I'll bet my eye he got you, you're as green as grass."

I wanted to cry. I felt such an idiot! I'd been humiliated and ripped off. I didn't know what I was doing, and everybody seemed to be able to tell. And all I had to show for it was ten pounds. I opened my mouth, ready to tell them to stick it – tell them all to stick it. The brothel, the club, the billionaires, everyone. But before I could speak, I felt something warm press against my hand. It was a cup of tea.

"I don't know how you like it," Destiny said. "I can put sugar in, if you want."

"It's fine," I said, surprised by the warmth in her tone.

"And don't let that old slapper Ruby over there give you any shit about Geoffrey. Her first time with him, he did her up the shitter and came on her face, then he said he'd forgotten his wallet! Silly cow forgot to get the money up front. And God knows, it's been an age since she was as green as grass!"

All three women were laughing, Ruby most of all.

"Sit your arse down, love," Ruby said, patting the

couch. "You're in the club, now."

I sat down, and realised that I actually felt okay. These women, that I had judged and written off, were just women like me – doing whatever it took. I was just luckier than them, that was all. I sipped my tea, and hoped that the next punter would be better than Geoffrey.

Hours later, I was exhausted. The shift had been busier than Destiny had predicted, and over the course of the six hours, I had seen eight punters. Only Geoffrey had tried to rip me off, but all the others had been just as demanding. And frankly, just as repulsive. They'd all seemed to want one end of the scale or the other, either a blow job or a full service. Mentally, I totted up my earnings as I bent over the bed. Five blowjobs at fifteen pounds each, less the five pounds I'd been cheated out of, made seventy pounds. I'd soon learned that they all wanted me to swallow – that seemed to be part of the attraction.

My second punter had wanted everything up to and including anal. That had netted me thirty pounds, as had my second-to-last customer. With the guy who was currently drilling my pussy, I was set to leave with £160. He'd paid for anal, even though it seemed as if he was trying to finish inside my pussy. There would be no refund, however. It was the most money I had ever earned in one day, and I felt that I had worked for every penny of it.

I was on the home stretch – once this guy had finished, all I had to do was service Mr Yellow and I was done. I had to remember not to wash before I left, either. Davina had been clear on that. I was confident that the shift had been humiliating enough, too. It was all going to be okay.

I felt the man pull out of my pussy. The man - Jesus

70

Christ, I don't even know his name. The head of his cock pressed against my asshole and I groaned internally. I was still sore from the last punter, whose dick had been in my ass less than an hour ago. And this one was bigger. I managed to twist my cries into moans of ecstasy as he roughly shoved its way into me and started pounding. Finish! Just finish! I willed, wanting it to be over. I knew from his grunts that he was very close. I moaned louder, hoping to egg him on.

But before I could react, before I even understood what was happening, he had pulled out. Snapping off the condom, he whirled around the bed, grabbing my head and holding it steady. Hot, sticky ropes of cum pumped onto my face. I was covered – completely spattered. Cum was dripping onto my bare breasts as I knelt on the bed, frozen in horror. It wasn't the act itself, frankly I'd rather have it on my face then have to swallow it. It was that he was the last punter, and I couldn't wash it off. There was no way around it – Mr Yellow would have had a clear view of what happened. I was fairly sure by now that I had worked out where the spy hole was.

The nameless punter dressed quickly and said his goodbyes, thanking me for the good time. He had closed the door behind him, and within seconds there was a knock.

"Come on now, love," Destiny yelled. "Next shift is here, I need that room."

I quickly dressed. Somehow, the tacky whore outfit didn't seem as bad as I'd initially thought. Probably because I'd spent half the day naked. And it was nothing, compared to having to go out there with a face full of cum. I separated out Destiny's money from the pile. Hopefully I could get out quickly and with no questions asked. Because how the fuck would I answer them?

When I got to the reception, Destiny, Ruby and Angel – the other older woman – were nowhere to be seen. But two people were sitting on the couches, a man and a woman. Fuck! The woman was presumably working the next shift, looking at her outfit. The man was her first punter of the evening.

"You done with the room?" she said.

"Yes," I said, turning away from her to drop Destiny's cut behind the counter.

"Come on, then," she said to the punter, practically dragging him down the hallway. I heard them collapse laughing, and I knew that they had seen my face.

"Goodbye!" I shouted, to no one in particular, and hurried down the stairs. I couldn't get out of there quick enough. The clapped-out taxi was waiting for me, the chauffeur ready to open the door for me. I couldn't look him in the eye, I didn't want to see the expression on his face. I knew he would be perfectly composed and neutral, pretending he didn't see it all, and somehow that was worse. Once more, I clambered into the back of the cab, and once more, there he was. Mr Yellow. I went to take my previous seat, the one opposite him.

"No you don't," he said. "Over here, next to me. Well, how much money did you make?" I took a seat as the cab moved off.

"£160," I said. Why was he asking? We both knew that he knew exactly how much money I'd made, and what I'd done to make it.

"It should have been £165 though, shouldn't it? But that first one had your number. Did you like it, swallowing his cum for free?"

"No," I said quietly.

"What about if he had paid you? Would you have liked swallowing his cum then?"

"No," I whispered. I was acutely aware that the chauffeur could hear the conversation, and that just seemed to make everything ten times worse.

"You must have liked it. You swallowed another four

loads after that. Earned yourself twenty quid." He smiled nastily. "I guess that means you're wearing a fiver's worth of spunk on your face, you fucking whore."

He placed a meaty hand high on my bare thigh.

"You want to earn another fiver, then?"

"No."

His fingers dug into my flesh, painfully. "I think you do," he said. "Say it."

"I want to earn another fiver," I said dully.

"And how do you want to earn it? Tell me exactly what you will do for five pounds," he said, grinning evilly.

I was determined not to cry. Forget trying to hide my humiliation – that was pointless. I was so utterly ashamed. But I didn't want to give him that last, final satisfaction of seeing the tears roll down my cum stained cheeks. "I will swallow your cum for five pounds," I said, staring down at the floor.

He slapped my thigh, gleefully. "You hear that?" he called to the chauffeur. "This dirty cow want to swallow my cum. Pull over."

I looked around in alarm as the car slowed, pulling into the curb. The street that we were on was in the heart of London, and there were tourists swarming around everywhere. Was he going to make me suck his cock right here in the cab? Anyone could look in and see us. Already, the taxi was attracting attention from would-be passengers. He reached into his pocket, pulling out a baseball cap and a pair of sunglasses. Smirking, he put them on. Shit! If he was disguising himself, then that was exactly what he had in mind. But it was so, so much worse than that…

He sprang out of the cab, pulling me with him. We were standing on the pavement, surrounded by people. My whorish outfit was on display, and I felt like I was naked. Those closest to us could see the dried cum on my face, too. I could hear whispers, and laughter. He leaned back against the taxi.

"Get on your knees," he said, coldly.

I did as he asked. It's just a few minutes, I thought wildly. A few minutes, and it will all be over. I've come this far. I could see his cock straining against the zipper of his jeans. Quickly, I pulled it out, desperate to get it over and done with. I heard somebody gasp. The passers-by were no longer passing by. They'd all stopped to watch the show. I began to suck his dick, just like I had sucked Geoffrey's dick, trying to do it well in the hope that he'd cum quickly. Mr Yellow was much bigger, though, and I was struggling to take him all in my mouth.

"Fucking hell, look at that bitch go! Why does nobody ever suck my cock like that?"

The voice came from the crowd, and was met with cheers and cat-calls.

"Maybe she'll suck yours next!" somebody yelled back.

A bright light flashed, startling me into looking over. A tourist was taking pictures of me. Countless others were filming me on their mobile phones. Mr Yellow started to thrust, ramming his cock down my throat. The crowd began to chant.

"Deep Throat! Deep Throat! Deep Throat!"

I couldn't help myself any longer. The tears that had been threatening all day finally started. I looked up at Mr Yellow as he face-fucked me, and I knew that he had been waiting for this moment. He started to cum, thick ropes filling my mouth for the sixth time that day. The crowd cheered ecstatically. He pulled out.

"Did you swallow it?"

I nodded, unable to speak.

"Show me."

I opened my mouth, showing him that I had

swallowed his load. He pulled a five pound note out of his pocket and crumpled it into my mouth. The crowd began to applaud wildly. He climbed back into the taxi, and I followed him, the banknote still in my mouth.

"Leave that in your mouth, and shut the fuck up," he said, deliberately sitting away from me. "Drop her back at the club," he called to the chauffeur. "I've got a gig to go to next."

The journey back to the club was only a few minutes. I sat in silence, money in my mouth, fat tears slowly rolling down my cheeks. It was over.

True to his word, Mr Yellow dumped me outside the Belgravia mansion, before speeding off into the night. The street was dark and deserted, and for that I was grateful. I pushed at the door – it was unlocked. Quietly, I slipped inside. All I wanted to do was get back to my room without seeing anybody. I nearly made it.

"Hey! Wait for me!" The whisper came out of the dark, behind me. I turned, and there was James. The smile on his face faded, as he saw the state of me. Once more, I began to cry, but this time it wasn't silent, dignified tears. It was full-on sobbing.

"Shh! Someone will hear you," he said, bundling me into my room and closing the door behind him. "It's okay, it's okay." He tried to hug me, but I pushed him away, running to the bathroom. He followed me.

"Go away! I don't want you to see me like this," I sobbed.

"Don't be silly," he said. "I know what this place is. You've been out with that music twat." He went to embrace me again, and this time I let him. He smelled fresh and clean, and I was suddenly aware of how scuzzy and gross I was.

"I need to get cleaned up," I said. "You should go."

"I'm not leaving you like this," he said firmly. "I'll

leave when I know that you're okay. Clean yourself up, and wash it all away. Everything – the experience, the memory. Let it all go down the drain, where it belongs. I'll wait out here for you."

I did as he said, and got into the shower. As the warm water cascaded down over me, I thought about what he had said – about washing it all away. And to my surprise, I found that I was washing it away. With every minute that passed, I felt better. The horrible, horrible day was fading and starting to feel like a bad dream. When I finally stepped back into the bedroom, wrapped in a fluffy white towel, I almost felt like myself.

"Better?"

"Actually, yes," I said. "But…"

"But what?" His eyes were filled with concern.

"But you don't have to, well, that is – if you want to stay a while, I don't mind." I was stumbling over my words, but it was true. I didn't want him to leave just yet. We'd barely spoken on the other occasions that we met, but yet I felt something, a strong attraction. It was almost magnetic. He probably didn't feel the same way, especially not after seeing me in such a state tonight, and knowing how I got that way. But I didn't care. I was too tired to think about it deeply. I just knew I wasn't ready for him to disappear into the dark just yet.

He smiled. "I have time, I can stay and visit for a little while. And you have snacks, too. I'm starving."

He was right. There was a tray of food on the table – cheese and crackers and fruit. I suddenly realised how hungry I was. I hadn't eaten since breakfast! Together, we fell on the tray, stuffing ourselves with food. Unable to speak with our mouths full, we exchanged smiles as we pigged out, until there was nothing left. It was... fun. Just ordinary, flirty fun. But we weren't in an ordinary situation. I had to know.

"James," I said, hesitantly.

"Elizabeth?" he replied. It was a shock, to hear my real name after all the fake ones. A nice shock, though. I'd have a new name, in the morning. I took a deep breath, screwing up my courage.

"Do you think that I'm..." I couldn't finish.

"That you're what?" he asked, frowning.

"A massive slut," I said. "For doing this, I mean. Joining the club."

He smiled, slowly. "You care, about what I think," he said softly. "That's good to hear, because I care about what you think too. And no, I don't think that you're a massive slut. I actually think that you're..." He brushed his thumb along my lower lip. "Kind of amazing."

My heart soared. He liked me, he actually liked me! Despite it all, the club and the circumstances in the situation, he felt the same magnetic force that was drawing us together. I gazed into his clear blue eyes. He was still stroking my lip, his hand warm and gentle on my face. In perfect synchronicity, we leaned in. But just as our lips were about to touch, the bedroom door slammed into the wall!

Davina was standing in the doorway, her face a cold mask of fury.

"GET. OUT. NOW." she spat.

Fear clutched at my heart. Was I about to lose everything that I'd worked for? And was I about to lose James?

AZURE

"GET. OUT. NOW."

Davina was glaring at James. He looked at me
nervously.

"I'll make this okay," he said, "if it comes back on
you."

"You won't need to," Davina snapped. "I'll protect
her. Just get out, you idiot."

James squeezed my hand, and got to his feet. Davina
pointedly stepped aside, holding the door open. As he
stepped out into the corridor, he turned to look at me,
mouthing later, later. Luckily, Davina didn't see. She
was already frowning at me as she slammed the door in
his face. I braced myself. I wasn't sure what I'd done,
exactly, but clearly it was something terrible.

"What in God's name was he doing in here?" Davina
said, sinking into the chair that James had just vacated.
Her tone had changed from anger to a weary despair,
which was only marginally less terrifying.

"We were just talking. I saw him on my way in, and
he came with me," I said. I didn't want to tell her how

upset I'd been when James found me. It sounded like my place at the club was in enough jeopardy already, without adding fuel to the fire. My fear was starting to give way to anger, though. How was I to know?

"I didn't know it wasn't allowed. I knew I couldn't bring outsiders in, but James works here. And this place is hardly a bloody nunnery, is it?"

She looked at me incredulously.

"He works here? James? You call him James, and he works here? Is that what he told you?"

"He told me his name was James," I said. "He didn't exactly say that he worked here, but he must do, surely? Why would he be here otherwise?"

Davina sank back in the chair, letting out a long, dramatic sigh.

"Sometimes, Azure, I forget how bloody naive you are."

"Azure?"

"Your new name. I haven't had chance to tell you it yet, but it's Azure."

I was relieved. If I had a new name, it meant I wasn't about to be turfed out. But Azure, though…

"There's not really that many names that mean blue," Davina smirked. She seemed to be calming down a little. My mind was filled with thoughts of James, though. He had seemed honest and trustworthy, but Davina seemed to be insinuating that he wasn't who he said he was. Not that he had really said much about himself – I'd filled in the blanks myself.

"What you mean, naive? What have I failed to understand? Has James lied to me?"

"No," she said. "Not technically, anyway. James is his real name. It's just that, well, you're not supposed to call him that. I know that sounds really 'nobles and peasants', but it's just the way it's always been. The rule dates back decades."

"What, I'm supposed to be all formal with the male staff? Since when? On my first day, Rose told me to call the butler John. I call you Davina. But I supposed to call James, then?"

She raised an eyebrow. "You're supposed to call him… Mr Orange."

What? No! Surely not…

"He's one of the billionaires? He… he doesn't…" I was lost for words.

"He doesn't look old and rich, you mean?"

"Well, yes. He's young, and he just seems - I don't know - ordinary." I felt a flash of guilt, describing James as ordinary. He was anything but.

"I can see what you mean," Davina said. "He is young, for a billionaire. He made some sort of computer app thing, and there was a website or something. Not really my cup of tea at all, to be honest, but it seems that I'm in the minority. He sold his company for a fortune, and as I understand it he's working on another one, now. He wants to see if lightning can strike twice."

"I'm so surprised," I said. "Mr Red and Mr Purple, they just seem to have an air of wealth about them. Like they were entitled, but in a nice way. James isn't like that all, he seems more… humble."

"Stop calling him James!" Davina hissed. "He does seem different to the others, though. It's a miracle, really. A lot of young men in his position act like complete arseholes." She seemed to realise that praising James wasn't doing anything to diffuse the situation. "I don't really know him that well, though, maybe he is an arsehole. He certainly knows better than to be sniffing around here."

It came back to me then. When Davina had given me the rundown about the programme and the billionaires, she had told me that the current Mr Orange was new, and he had replaced the man that she had fallen in love with. That was why she worked here – The Prism Club had offered her a position after she dropped out of the programme.

"I know what you're thinking," I said, "and you don't need to worry. History isn't going to repeat itself, I promise."

"Good. Don't make the same mistake I did. If there is really something between you, it will still be there after you finish the programme. But now, you have to focus your efforts on getting through. We should start preparation for the next task."

"We? Are you actually going to help me, this time? You were uncharacteristically absent for the last one." I was annoyed. If Davina had prepared me better about what to expect with Mr Yellow, or even if she had just been there when I got back, James would never have ended up in my room. Obviously, I didn't dare say that to her, though.

"I know, I'm sorry. I thought it was for the best. I knew how rough it was going to be, but I also knew it would all be over fairly quickly. I didn't want you to give up, and if I told you beforehand about it, you would have turned tail and run."

It was true. There is no way that I would have agreed to being publicly face fucked in the centre of London. I felt a wave of horror, as I thought about all the cameras and phones that had recorded me.

"I'm probably all over the bloody Internet by now," I said.

"Hardly," Davina said. "That's the other thing that I couldn't tell you beforehand. If you had known, your reactions wouldn't have been genuine and he would have picked up on it. The whole street was closed off for the filming of a 'music video'. Those people – they weren't the general public. They were actors, well, extras really. As far as they know, it was all fake, you're an American child star trying to shed your wholesome image, and Mr Yellow is a lookalike."

I didn't know whether to hug her or hit her. The humiliation wasn't real – it had been real at the time – but not now. I still thought Mr Yellow was an obnoxious creep, but Davina was right. It was over and done with. I tried to remember what she had told me about the next one, but I was coming up blank. At the time, it had barely seemed real.

"So how do we prepare for Mr Blue?"

"Dr Blue, if you remember," she said chidingly.

Now it was my turn to smirk. "Oh yes, I remember now. He's the one that does your Botox."

"Don't mock, age will catch up with you too one day, and then you'll be begging to know my secrets."

She wasn't wrong. Even in her forties, she was impressively glamorous and put together. She could give any woman a run for their money.

"Dr Blue, well, he has very specific tastes. He doesn't play 'Doctors and Nurses' so much as 'Obstetrician and Post-partum Patient'. Don't worry, it's not his real life speciality. He's actually a neurosurgeon. But in his private life, he enjoys examining women that recently gave birth, messing about with lactation, that kind of thing."

"I hate to state the obvious here," I said, "but I am not in any way shape or form post-partum." I was feeling slightly smug, because I knew that she wasn't expecting me to know what the medical terms meant.

She snorted. "He doesn't want it realistic! Bleeding vaginas, cracked nipples and haemorrhoids – not his thing at all. He just pretends – compliments you on how well you've tightened up after the birth, stuff like that. And for god's sake, don't mention actual babies. The only thing that he insists on being real is the breast milk. So for that, we going to have to inject you with some hormones."

She must have seen the alarm on my face.

"It's perfectly safe. They take about three days to kick in, you'll see him on day four, and by the fifth day you'll be right as rain."

"So, you've done this, then? What was it like?"

"I barely remember it, so it can't have been that bad. I remember my tits being huge – I was devastated when they went back to normal. I was perhaps a little snappy, but no more than if it was that time of the month."

I hated to think what the snappy version of Davina was like. God knows, she was abrupt enough as it was. But the hormones didn't really sound that bad, so I was happy enough to go along with it. By the time she had finished injecting me, it felt like our relationship was back to normal after the James debacle. I knew better than to bring his name up again, but he was on my mind constantly. The main issue, of course, was that I would be expected to see him as part of the programme. I was worried about how that would play out. With all the other billionaires, our relationships had been distant and, despite the circumstances, quite formal. It was always very clear who was in charge – and that wasn't me. But what would that be like with James? We had connected, on a personal level. I didn't see how we could go back to the arrangement that the Prism Club embodied, but I didn't see what the alternative was either.

Secretly, in my heart of hearts, my hope was that my time with James would be simply a free pass to enjoy each other's company, but somehow I doubted the likelihood of that happening. After all, he'd signed up to this programme for a reason – it wasn't a dating agency. Davina hadn't told me much about what he was into sexually, just that it was a boss/secretary theme. That could be anything, I knew now. I wasn't the innocent, naive girl that I was on the day that I received that bottle of perfume. But there was no point dwelling on it. I didn't know, I couldn't ask, so I would just have to wait and see. In the meantime, Davina was right. I had to focus on what was in front of me.

The next few days were... strange. I didn't feel ill, exactly, from the hormones, but they were certainly having an affect. I found that my emotions were all heightened – I was quicker to anger, and quicker to tears. Physically, however, it wasn't that bad at all. My skin seemed more sensitive to touch, especially my breasts. The milk was coming in, and they were steadily getting bigger. I spent hours staring at myself in the mirror. It was fascinating. This is what I would look like if I had a boob job, I thought to myself. Not many people women get to see that in real life, I suppose. Genuine pregnant women look pregnant – they have the rounded tummy as well. but my belly had stayed flat. Well, not flat, but no bigger than it had been before the hormones. On the day before I was due to see Dr Blue, I was issued with some new underwear.

I was glad, because my vastly oversized boobs were no longer fitting into the bras that I had. But when I opened the package, I was surprised. Instead of the lovely, flattering, delicate lingerie I had grown to expect from the Prism Club, this stuff was horrible. There was a flesh coloured bra, very utilitarian and featureless, with matching granny-pants style knickers. The bra must have weighed two pounds.

"I know," Davina had said, when I opened it. "You're to put the bra on now, and not take it off until you're with Dr Blue."

"Why?" I said.

"Because it's thick. He doesn't want you playing with your boobs and nipples, and letting the milk out. He wants to be there when it happens, be the one that does all that for the first time."

By this point, I knew better than to be surprised. I was learning that sexuality was a much wider and diverse thing than I had ever previously imagined. If that's what he likes, I thought, then that's what he gets. The bra was awful, though. Wearing it, I could actually pinch my breast and not feel it.

"What about having a shower?" I asked.

"Wear it in the shower, too," Davina said. "Although you'll have to get up early, to make sure the damn thing is dries out in time. You'll be seeing him tomorrow afternoon. I'll walk you to his room. And don't worry," she said, looking at me, "this one won't be like the last one. He's pretty out there, but he's a nice guy."

I was relieved by this. And to be honest, it did sound kind of fun – I was fascinated by the thought of my body being able to actually produce food, of sorts. All it had ever done before was dispose of food, I thought wryly. The rest of the day passed in an iron-breasted blur. I got up early, as instructed, took a shower, and then spent the rest of the morning lounging around in my underwear, so that the heavy fabric could dry. Davina had trusted me to do my own make up, because 'it was very easy' and apparently I 'had to learn sooner or later'. The look required was a minimal one, nothing fancy, and when I had finished I was actually quite proud of myself. It looked good – not the flawless artistry that Davina would have produced – but nevertheless, I was quite pleased with myself.

When Davina arrived to collect me, she didn't comment on it, which I knew was the highest compliment she was capable of giving – no actual criticism. As we made our way down the corridors, I was surprised to find that I was feeling pretty enthusiastic. Davina ran through a last minute briefing.

"It's almost like acting, really. Just remember your

role. You've recently given birth, only that, nothing more. Don't even say the word baby - it's a complete mood killer. You are having your first check-up since the birth. The purpose of the check-up is to make sure that all your bits and pieces are fully functional, mostly from a sexual point of view, of course. The vibe is more deferential, then anything. Really, you'll mostly be just telling him how things feel. And how do they feel?"

"They feel good," I said, smiling. I was getting the hang of this.

"Okay, this is the door," she said. "I don't know how long you'll be, so just make your own way back after. Have fun with this one – just don't fly into a hormone induced rage, and you'll be fine."

She kissed me on the cheek, and bustled away at her usual brisk pace. I knocked on the door.

"Come in," a man's voice said.

I opened the door. For some reason, I'd been expecting a room like Mr Red's dungeon – mostly because I hadn't really seen many of the rooms in this enormous place. But it looked exactly like a normal doctor's office. There was a desk with a chair on each side, an examination bed, and all the other paraphernalia that you tend to see. There was even an eyesight testing chance on the wall. The man behind the desk was perhaps in his mid-fifties. He was handsome, though, for his age. He was wearing a white coat, of course, and he had a salt-and-pepper beard and glasses. He looked every inch a well-respected medical professional.

"Ah, Miss Azure," he said. "Come in, you're right on time."

I sat in the patient chair, and waited.

"Now, my notes tell me you've recently given birth, and now you need a full physical to make sure that everything is in tiptop condition. Is that correct?"

"Yes, Dr," I said. He seemed pleased.

"Well then, dear, if you want to just pop your outer clothes off for me, and hop up there on the bed, we can have a look."

Remarkably, he indicated towards a fabric screen, presumably for me to get undressed behind. I was amused at this attempt to protect my modesty – we both knew where this appointment was headed – but I supposed it added to the realism for him. I stepped behind the screen and took off my dress. It was a simple, plain shift dress. Classic, rather than sexy or seductive. I liked it, though. It wasn't the kind of thing I would have worn prior to the Club – I'd have thought it too 'grown-up' - but it was a style that I thought I would probably embrace, once I had finished here. I slipped off my shoes, which left me wearing only the hateful underwear. Immediately, I felt a million times less sexy, but when I stepped out from behind the screen, I saw his eyes light up. As I sat on the bed, he came over, hooking a stethoscope into his ears.

"I'll listen to your heartbeat first," he said, pressing the end of the stethoscope onto my left breast. I jumped – it was cold. He listened for a moment, and as he did, he stroked a finger along the inside of my thigh.

"Good, that's all fine and healthy." He said. "But I noticed that, when I touched your thigh, your heartbeat sped up a little. To have such a reaction from so little stimulus doesn't necessarily indicate a problem, but it's important that we investigate it thoroughly. I'm going to attach this here–" he said, snapping what looked like a metal cuff around my wrist, "and now this device will monitor your heart rate. It transmits the information to the screen over there." He turned on a monitor, and on the screen there was a small, white circle. As I watched, the circle would expand, turning a pinkish colour, and then shrink back. I realised that each expansion represented a beat of my heart. Presumably, as my heartbeat sped up, the circle would get bigger and redder. I hoped that whatever he was going to do was genuinely exciting – there was no way to fake a heartbeat!

"Now, what I need you to do is kneel up on the examination table, so that you're on your hands and knees, facing the monitor. Yes, that's it."

The examination table was high, and in that position, my bottom was level with his chest. He moved around the bed, so that he was standing behind me. I a prickle of anticipation, unable to see what he was doing, and immediately the pulsing circle on the monitor began to speed up. If he noticed, he didn't comment.

"Now, we'll get rid of these," he said, sliding the horrible knickers off, "and I'll perform the visual inspection."

I couldn't see him, but I knew that he was very close to me. I could feel his soft, warm breath against my rapidly moistening pussy. It was the completely unknown element that was turning me on so much. I was prone, and vulnerable, and I didn't know what was coming next. It was insanely exciting.

"Yes, all looks well externally. Internally, though, remains to be seen. I'm going to use what we call a speculum, to hold you open and have a look. Normally, in this situation, one would use a lubricant. However, the artificial chemicals could interfere with other tests, so instead I will apply some stimulation to create the situation naturally."

His phrasing was very clinical, but I understood what he meant. He was going to get me wet. Not that I needed it – he must have been able to see that I was already there. I felt his finger delicately trace along the lips of my pussy, down towards my clit. Involuntarily, I let out a moan as he began to massage the sensitive bud, swirling the tip of his finger around and around. After a couple of delicious moments, though, he took his finger away. I was frustrated – I didn't want it to stop. The urge to put my hand between my legs, and carry on what he had started was almost overwhelming, but I knew that it wasn't what he wanted.

"That's much better," he said. He slid the cold speculum into my pussy, opening it. There was a pause, so presumably he was peering in. I wanted to howl with frustration – the speculum was doing nothing for me. I was all revved up, and I needed to get off.

"Yes, that's all fine too," he said, removing the speculum. "And now for the arousal monitoring. I'm going to insert a device that will provide some sexual stimulation – not too much, mind – and track how it affects your heart. We don't want you having a heart attack, keeling over and dying the next time you have an orgasm, do we?"

The sexual stimulation sounded good - I was almost trembling with the need for relief. I felt him slide something cold, hard and solid into my pussy. It was big, and thick. Already, the monitor was responding – and then he switched the thing on! It began to vibrate inside me, and the feeling was amazing. It was hitting every pleasure point I had. I'd never used a vibrator before, and I realised that I had been missing out for all these years. I could feel my orgasm building, and I started to push back against the instrument, wanting as much stimulation as possible. The circle on the monitor had turned from pink to a bright red, and it was pulsating rapidly.

"Yes, now, that's quite enough of that," he said, abruptly removing the wondrous device. No! "And really, Miss Azure, I'd prefer it if you try to remain still."

I took the hint. Clearly, I was only going to be allowed to cum when he wanted it, not when I wanted it. I felt an irrational flash of rage – no doubt hormone induced – and managed to choke it down. After all, I was supposed to be here for him, not me. I gritted my teeth, and waited to see what would happen next.

"Now, the next test," he said. "We need to make sure that the wall between your anus and vagina hasn't been damaged. It's a very delicate piece of tissue, you see. Now that you have sufficiently lubricated the first instrument, we can use it anally."

I felt the instrument press against my asshole, and gasped. It was still turned off. Slowly, he slid it inside me. It was bigger than anything I'd taken up there before, and I was aware of how stretched I I felt.

"And the second instrument…"

The second one, as big as the first, was being slowly inserted into my pussy. I was completely full, and breathless with desire.

"Now, when I turn them on, they will measure the thickness and quality of the tissue that separates them. It doesn't take very long to complete the reading, don't worry" he said.

Jesus Christ! If he cut me off again, before I could cum, I was going to go insane. He turned the machines on...

The two together meant that the pleasure was more than doubled – it was infinitely better! The huge, hard machines pulsed and vibrated, and my pussy and ass felt as if they were fizzing over. I managed to stay still, as he had instructed, but I was unable to keep quiet. I gasped and moaned, completely lost in the moment. I wanted to cum, cum as quickly as possible, before he could stop me. He hadn't specifically said that I wasn't allowed to orgasm, so I was going to go for it! But the damned heart rate monitor was giving me away again. It was speeding up, flashing deep red, betraying me. Please, please, I thought to myself. I need this. I felt as if I was going to explode.

Dr Blue strolled around from behind me, up to the monitor.

"Well, look at this," he said. "It seems as if you're very close to climax. That could be dangerous, of course. As a medical professional, it would be irresponsible of me to let you continue."

I couldn't help myself. "No! Please don't stop it. I… I want to…"

"I am a medical professional, Miss Azure, but I'm also a man. And I know that you young ladies have your ways of distracting a man from the task at hand," he said, turning to face me.

My head was level with his chest, and I could see the tell-tale bulge pressing against the clinical white coat. I didn't hesitate for a second. I quickly unfastened a couple of the lab coat buttons, and his cock sprang free - his trousers had been unzipped the whole time. I took him into my mouth, trying to go slowly with him, so that he didn't cum too soon – cum before I did. But it was difficult to control myself. I was a mass of sensation and emotion, and all I wanted to do was suck this man's cock, as the machines buzzed inside me. Greedily, I took more and more of his length, pushing him further and further down into my throat. He didn't touch me, or encourage me, but he didn't stop me either. I knew he was enjoying it, though. I could taste the pre-cum on my tongue as I licked the head of his cock.

The pleasure was unbearable, and I could hold out no longer. I started to cum, twitching and spasming on the examination table. His cock in my mouth was the only physical contact I had, and I sucked it harder and harder as each wave of pleasure flooded my senses. I let out a series of what would have been loud cries, had they not been stifled by his dick. With each burst of sensation, I thrust my head mouth right down the length of him, gagging and choking as he filled me.

Finally, my orgasm was over. He surprised me by pulling out of my mouth – I'd expected him to continue until he came, too. But instead, he moved back down to the machines and began to remove them from my holes. His rock hard dick was still exposed, though, and I knew we weren't done yet.

"Well, Miss Azure," he said. "We seem to have drawn a conclusion, there. I'm pleased to tell you that your heart is in full working order, and you need not fear complications from sexual arousal. In fact, your entire system is healthy and well. You can sit back on the table, now, and I'll take this – we won't be needing it any more." He removed the bracelet monitor from my wrist. I swung my legs round, so that I was sitting back where I had started, on the table. He quickly dumped all the equipment on his desk, and came back over to me. His cock was still hard, and I had the urge to reach out and touch it – how much I had changed in such a short period of time!

"Now, we need to have a look at those breasts. You have been wearing the support garment as instructed?"

"Yes, Dr," I said.

"And how has that been, any discomfort or pain?"

"No, Dr," I said. "I haven't felt anything at all."

"Excellent, excellent," he said. "Now, if you could just remove the support garment..."

I unhooked the heavy bra, and immediately it fell away. God, it had been heavy! But I hadn't realised how much support and compression it had been giving me. Finally released, my breasts were huge – full and swollen. And I had the most peculiar sensation in them. They ached, as if they needed to release. It was uncomfortable, and my instinct was to squeeze and manipulate them, to ease the feeling. Somehow, I kept my hands by my side. It was like trying not to scratch an itch, and I was pretty sure he knew it, too. I felt the rage flash up again – I thought he got off on medical things and birth stuff, not torturing people!

"Yes, they are very engorged. Your milk has come in."

He placed his hand on the underside of my left breast, and lifted it, and then he did the same with the right. He seemed to be weighing them. The ache and the need grew deeper, and I gritted my teeth once more.

"Now, I need you to keep your hands right where they are, down by your sides. I'm going to see how your breasts react to stimulation."

Thank God! My breasts were aching for stimulation. I felt that they would react by exploding, and I welcomed it! But his hands moved away from them, down to my thighs. He pushed them apart slightly and cupped my sex, gently stroking my clit. I felt a wetness on my nipples, and looked down in surprise – beads of milk was starting to appear! It was fascinating, but it wasn't enough. I needed to empty them completely. Somewhere in the back of my mind, I wondered if this was how a man felt when he needed to cum. Did his balls ache, like I was doing?

"Good, good," he murmured, almost to himself. He moved his hands back to my breasts, cupping them and using his thumbs to rub against my rock hard nipples, smearing the beads of milk across them.

"Oh yeah, that is so fucking hot," he said, dropping the doctor role-play - this was the core of what he enjoyed. He was no longer the neutral medical professional. He was simply a horny, lust driven man.

He started to squeeze my breasts, forcing my milk from them. It was what I wanted – a small part of what I wanted – and I could feel my breath becoming shorter and shallower. He bent his head, and licked the milk from my nipple. I felt a spark of electricity go straight down to my pussy at the flick of his tongue. I gasped.

"Over here," he said roughly, picking me up around my waist and stumbling over to his doctor chair. He sat down in it, and then I was straddling him, face to face. He lifted my hips again, shifting my position, and just like that his hard cock was inside me. He slid his hands up to my shoulder blades, supporting me as I leaned back. I started to slide up and down his cock slowly, and he bent his head towards me.

This time, he didn't lick or tease. He sucked, switching between my two huge breasts, giving me the relief I craved. But it wasn't just a relief from discomfort, though. It was a sexual pleasure - completely new and different to anything I had experienced. Having my breasts and nipples played with felt amazing, but never enough to get me off. But this – this feeling of being emptied, all the pressure being relieved, it was like something I'd never imagined. He was fucking me, and that felt good too, but I knew that even if he was only sucking on my tits, I would cum hard.

He had started to take over, doing all the work. It was no longer me riding him – he was slamming himself up into me, going faster and faster as he sucked harder and harder. As he sucked on one breast, he would squeeze the other hard in his fist, and it was a delicious mix of pleasure and pain. I started to cum again, throwing my head back and screaming as the orgasm tore through me. I could feel my milk pumping out in spurts as I came and came, and that seemed to tip him over the edge. He was battering himself into my pussy, and I could feel the hot sticky ropes of cum started flood me as he moaned and groaned.

As soon as he had finished cumming, he lifted me up off his cock, sitting me on his desk. I smiled up at him, but my smile faded on my face. He looked… angry. I was confused – hadn't this been everything he wanted? He had certainly seemed to enjoy himself.

He stood up and stepped away from the desk, turning his back to me as he put his dick away and refastened the lab coat.

"You need to wear these for the next half-hour or so," he said, rummaging in a cupboard. The friendly doctor routine was gone, and he seemed thoroughly pissed off. I was annoyed. I had done everything he wanted. Was it my fault if he was ashamed of himself after sex? No, I thought, it bloody well wasn't!

"Okay," I said, deliberately omitting the title doctor. He brought the latest device over. I'd never seen one before, but it was pretty obvious what it was – an electric breast pump. He practically slammed the plastic cups onto my breasts, roughly strapping them in place.

"This will empty you out. When you're completely dry, turn it off and go back to your room. Thank you for your time."

And with that, he pressed a button on the machine, and walked out of the room. What the hell was that? I was furious. I'd done everything that I showed, and it had been good. He'd enjoyed it, I'd enjoyed it – it was all that it should be. But now I was sitting here, on my own, strapped up to a machine like a bloody cow!

The machine wasn't orgasmic, like his other devices. In fact, it was downright uncomfortable. Dr Blue didn't come back, and there was no sign of Davina either, although I wasn't expecting her. Alone, I sat and fumed, watching my milk filling the storage chamber.

After ten minutes or so, it had reduced to a trickle, and I could wait no longer. I switched it off and removed the contraption. Time to go. I looked at the ugly underwear on the floor. He can keep it, I decided. I would go commando under my dress. It was all he was keeping, though. There was a small sink in the corner, and I wasted no time emptying the milk chamber! If he was planning to get off on it, he was going to be severely disappointed, I thought viciously.

As I stalked along the corridors to my room, I found that my mood was getting worse, rather than better. I kept replaying the scene in my mind, imagining myself coming out with a variety of withering put-downs to Dr Blue. This just made me feel worse, though, because I knew deep down that in real life I would never have said any of them, even if I had been able to think of them in time. As I turned the corner to my room, I could see a figure, lounging against the door. Dr Blue, come to apologise? No. It was James.

"Hey there," he said, smiling easily. He looked down at me. "You seem to have something on your..."

I looked down. There were two dark patches on my dress, where the last of my milk had leaked through. This was the final straw!

"So?" I bit out. "What you want?"

"I just wanted to make sure you're okay, after the other night. You didn't get into any trouble, did you?"

I was seething, and here was a target for my rage. I knew that I could let out all my frustration and get away with it, and I'm ashamed to say that I let him absolutely have it.

"Trouble? And what if I had have got into trouble? How would this – you coming here again and hanging around – help with that trouble, exactly? It wouldn't. It would make it worse. Which makes me think that you're not here to check on me at all. You're not here for my own good, you're here for your own benefit."

"No! No... I..."

I shoved him out of the way. "Just fuck off!" I yelled at the top of my voice, wrenching open the door and stamping inside, slamming it behind me. The cheek of him! I flung myself down on the bed, like a child having a temper tantrum. He didn't knock on the door, or try to come in. Somehow, even though I had told him to fuck off, that made me even more angry. He clearly didn't care about me at all!

But, like all raging toddlers, I couldn't sustain my fury for too long. I only realised that I had drifted off to sleep when Davina woke me.

"How did it go?" she asked.

"Has he made a report?" I said. "It was… strange. He seemed to be really into it, but then afterwards he was angry. Really angry."

"Really? You surprise me, he's not normally like that. He's cleared you for progression, too. Tell me exactly what happened."

I went through the whole tale. Now that I had calmed down, I felt a bit embarrassed about how angry I'd been – I wasn't normally petty and spiteful. By the time I had reached the part where I tipped the milk down the sink, Davina was smirking.

"And according to you, I'm the bad-tempered one! I can see exactly what went wrong, and it wasn't your fault. He usually likes to stay in character all the way through, you see. The scene normally ends with him pumping the milk, and then the patient giving him a hand job, because she is so grateful for his medical expertise. He wasn't pissed off at you, he was pissed off at himself for losing control. It's a good thing, really. His recommendation was very positive."

I was so relieved, and so ashamed as well. I had just assumed that his anger was aimed at me, and I'd flown into a temper. Then I remembered the other thing I'd done in anger.

"There's something else, too," I said. "When I got back, James was waiting outside the door."

I wanted to cry. He had been waiting for me, to see if I was okay, and I'd been awful to him.

"What did you say to him?" Davina said, eyes narrowed.

"I told him to fuck off," I said.

"Good," Davina said. "That's exactly what I would have done, too. If he comes bothering you again, I'll deal with him myself."

I didn't want to tell her how I felt, that I was dying inside at the memory of his face when I had screamed at him. This was for the best.

"How will it work when it's his turn, though?" I asked.

"We'll see. If there's any more trouble out of him between now and then, I'll get him booted out of the programme. If he keeps his head down, I'll just remind him beforehand that he needs to keep it professional. It won't affect your progression either way, as long as you behave yourself."

"I will," I promised. I didn't really have an option, now. Not after the way I had treated him.

"I'm sure you know what I'm going to say next," Davina said, "but it's true, so I'm going to say it again. Put him out of your head. Your focus needs to be on the next assignment. It starts in a couple of days time, once all the hormones are out of your system. Nobody likes an moody diva on set!"

On set? I remembered – the next assignment was Mr Green. The porn king.

"I'm looking forward to this one," Davina smirked. "I'm going to give you a fabulous makeover – the classic porn star look. Fake tan, fake eyelashes, fake nails and fake hair. You'll be an absolute fire hazard!"

"Really? I'm not convinced that you're going to be able to pull that one off convincingly, at least not on me. I'm the least 'porn star' looking person in the world."

"Oh ye of little faith," she said confidently. "You have no idea about the range and extent of my powers. Besides, you're looking at it the wrong way. Azure could never be a porn star - she's a new mother with understated taste and a vile temper…"

I threw a pillow at her, laughing.

"But the woman that I'll be sending out is Jade, and Jade is a bombshell!"

Jade. My new name was Jade, and I was a porn star. I liked it. I'd lost James before I ever really had him, so all I really had now was myself. I'd never dared to admit it to myself before coming here, but I wanted to be sexy, and desired. I had always felt that I wasn't good enough, pretty enough, thin enough, confident enough. The Prism Club was opening my eyes, teaching me that anyone and everyone could be sexy and desirable if they embraced it, even me. I was going to embrace it all. I was going to be Jade.

JADE

Every time I passed the mirror, I did a double take. Who was that girl in the glass? She looked like me, but different. Maybe a cousin, perhaps, one that had grown up in a different family – the kind of happy, well-off family that breeds confident, successful children. Most of the transformation had happened over the last couple of days. I was leaving Azure, the simple and classical girl behind to become Jade, the bombshell. The blonde bombshell, in fact.

When Davina had told me that I was going blonde, I was worried. I'd never dyed my hair, not even in the awkward teenage years. To be honest, it had never seemed worthwhile – I'd accepted my fate as a Plain Jane long before. I had never had anything other than my pale, mousy, no-colour brown hair. So when I pictured going blonde, I pictured a brassy, deep-fried frizz, like the woman I had seen at the massage parlour. Brothel hair.

But with her usual combination of gentle reassurance and ruthless determination, Davina pushed ahead and applied the highlights two days ago, and I loved it. It was subtle, and natural looking, but somehow it made me look more polished, more together and more... noticeable.

Before the Prism Club, being noticeable would have been the worst thing that I could have imagined. I didn't want people to notice me, I wanted to hide away. But my confidence had come along in leaps and bounds since then. If I could survive giving a public blow job in Leicester bloody Square, being noticeable would be a walk in the park. And that was good, because tonight was the night. I was going to become a porn star

Well, not an actual star. I'd been assured that the editing process would make sure that I wasn't recognisable as me, so I wouldn't have fans stopping me on the street and asking for my autograph any time soon. But it would be out there, the video, on the Internet for anybody to watch.

I was torn between excitement and nerves. Excitement, because it was something that I never believed would happen – I would be the object of desire for hundreds, maybe even thousands of men. And nerves, because I had spent the last few days watching the previous videos...

The only thing I had really known about porn was the stereotypes – the pizza delivery man, the pool boy, the plumber. They come round, fuck the horny housewife, and go on their merry way. But, like so many things, there was a whole world which I was completely unaware of. There was porn for everything, it seemed. I focused on Mr Green's films, though. They were the ones I needed to watch, the style that I would be making, the billionaire I would be pleasing.

Each one was different, but one theme ran through them all - dominant men and submissive women. One had been very much like my experience with Mr Red –

the dungeon, the cuffs, the spanking, but some had been different – girls trying new things, girls paying off their bills with sex, orgies, even a medical play video. So many elements were the same as my experiences in the Prism Club, and I wondered which had inspired which. I couldn't figure out which one was the girl who went on to win an Oscar, no matter how hard I tried. Davina's only input was to assure me in no uncertain terms that her video was not among the collection.

I had no idea what my storyline was to be. All Davina knew was that every video Mr Green shot was different, so I could rule out everything I saw. That didn't help me at all – I'd come a long way, but I was still a sexual ignoramus. I had no idea what remained, and it was the unknown that gave me the nerves.

There was another thing bothering me, too. After this one, Mr Orange was next. And Mr Orange was James. I hadn't seen him since I'd slammed the door in his face, but despite my best efforts he had been on my mind constantly. It was stupid - I barely knew him - but I had felt such an instant, life-changing connection, and I knew he felt the same. Between the Prism Club rules and my own stupid temper though, it was doomed. Nevertheless, I would still have to see him, have to touch him, have to sleep with him and fulfil his every sexual desire...

I shook my head, annoyed that my thoughts had turned away from tonight and back to James, again. To distract myself, I examined the other transformations that Davina had insisted upon. I didn't think I would be keeping anything apart from the hair.

I had false eyelashes, and I hated them with a passion. They looked good, yes, but they were driving me insane. I could see them constantly, and feel them every time I blinked. I longed to rip them off, but Davina had promised to attach the second set with a stapler, and

I only half-believed she was joking.

She'd given me a full set of shiny acrylic nails, too. I had mixed emotions about them – I liked how they looked, but then I tried to pick something up. It was as if my fingers were hobbled – I could barely work them. Davina had scoffed, of course.

"For god's sake, they're not even that long," she had said. "Look at mine, and I manage just fine. You'll get used to them, and after that you won't be able to live without them. Mark my words."

The fake tan was another matter, though. Even Davina agreed it looked terrible, but apparently it was necessary to look good on camera. Some fake tans looked good, she had told me, and I shouldn't be put off for life. My fake tan, however, wasn't one of the ones that looked good. It was one of the ones that bodybuilders use to highlight the muscles. It was... orange. And of course, every time I thought about the word orange, I thought about Mr Orange, and then I was back to square one. I couldn't wait for it to fade.

Overall though, I had to admit that I looked the part completely, something that I had never thought would happen. I been subjected to another brutal waxing, this one even more thorough than the last. I understood why, though. I had seen the videos - I knew how close the camera got.

It was nearly time. I dressed quickly in the clothes that had been laid out for me. It was strange – of all the outfits that I had worn in my time here, this one was the most similar to my old, original clothes. A plain T-shirt, and a pair of sweat pants with trainers. Nicer and more expensive than my gear, obviously, but even so, it was a marked departure from the expected style. When I had queried it, Davina had explained that the studio would be dressing me for the shoot, and in the meantime, they didn't want me to get marks from tight fitting clothes or underwear. Hence the casual attire.

When the chauffeur came to collect me, I still couldn't make eye contact with him, not after the last time I'd seen him. He was neutral and professional as always, though. The shoot was in a warehouse just outside London. From the outside, it looked like any other warehouse – just a dingy storage place – but when I walked in, it was like walking onto a Hollywood set. There were high-end, technical looking cameras and lights, and maybe seven or eight sets that looked exactly like real rooms – bedrooms, kitchens and so on. A man walked over to greet me, and I knew before he even opened his mouth that this would be Mr Green. Although he wasn't dressed flashily - in fact he was dressed down even more than I was - he had the confident, self-assured manner of somebody who knows his place in the world.

"You must be Jade," he said, in a warm California drawl. "It's great to have you here." He grabbed my shoulders and quickly leaned in, kissing both my cheeks before I knew what was happening.

"It's lovely to meet you too," I stammered. He wrapped an arm around my shoulder, leading me across the warehouse floor.

"Okay, I'll run through the scene with you, and then we'll get you into hair and make up. We'll start shooting in about an hour."

He led us over to a couple of camp chairs in the corner, and picked up a stack of notes.

"Now," he began, "For this one, we're going to go with a home invasion theme..." He caught the look of confusion on my face. "Burglars, as you Brits say. You're sleeping in your bed, the invaders break in, you fuck them, done. I'm looking for a gonzo vibe, so we're going with a one camera set-up."

I had literally no idea what the technical stuff meant,

so I just nodded and hoped I wouldn't be expected to comment. The theme confused me a little, though. All the other videos I had seen had been quite dark, but this one sounded like some sort of porno Sleeping Beauty storyline.

"I don't know if I fully understand," I said. "I just wake up and start getting it on with them?" In all his other films, there had been more of a story line.

He looked amused.

"No, honey. You really not seen any of this stuff before? The whole concept of the piece is that the woman – you – doesn't, well, she's not really into it at first. Of course, once it gets going, she's fucking loving it."

"So, it's like a rape scene?" I said.

"Dubious consent is the term used. Of course, that's just the story. If you're not happy you can plug at any time. You okay with that?"

"Sure," I said. The theme didn't bother me – in fact it sounded, well, kind of hot. My main concern was my acting skills – I wasn't really sure that I had any.

"Is there a script?" I asked.

"Not as such. I find that using a word-for-word, lined script can come off pretty wooden. I'll give you direction, and I'm looking to wrap it up in one take. That should get us a good result. I'll walk you through the opener of it now, and then use the time in make-up to get into the head space. You'll be great!"

I really hoped he was right.

"You're asleep in the bed. Guys come in – you'll hear them – but stay sleeping. They'll pull back the covers and look at you, you're still asleep. You can shift position a little – you don't wanna look like a corpse – but no rolling over or anything. And for fuck's sake, don't try and snore. There'll be some touching, you're still asleep. Then there's touching your clit. You're moaning in your sleep, eyes still closed, starting to wake up, starting to respond a little... and then boom! You wake up and see them. You're scared, screaming, they tell you to keep quiet, you're crying. You have to do what they say, and you do, but you're still crying and afraid. The scene plays out, we get the money shot – when the guys cum - and then we're done." He smiled proudly.

"But what about the rest of the scene? What do I do for that?" I said.

"Just react to what's happening. If you don't know what's coming, you'll be more natural. Don't look at the camera, don't think about anything outside of the role."

I could do that. Maybe. "Where are the other actors?"

"You won't see them until the scene. It makes it-"

"More natural?"

"Exactly!" He seemed pleased. "Go over through that door and get your hair and make-up done. Stay in your role. Stacy won't bother you, she doesn't speak English."

I headed over to the make-up room, trying to process all that he had said. You're asleep in bed. You wake up and there's strange men. You're scared and crying, I told myself, over and over. The woman in the make-up room, presumably Stacy, gestured wordlessly to a chair. As soon as I sat, she began to attack my face with brushes and sponges, moving my head about as she required. I was already wearing the ton of make-up that Davina had applied earlier, but clearly there was to be more. It was annoying, but it made it easier to stay in my mind. I pictured waking up in my old bed, in the tiny flat, and imagined how I would feel. I pictured my room at the Prism Club, and did the same.

Eventually, Stacy stopped mauling me and stepped away. I looked in the mirror and was shocked. She'd applied shading with a heavy hand, all over my face. Up close, I looked like a clown, but I could see how that, on camera, it would look better. The lines and contours subtly changed the shape of my face, and altered my features. Clearly, this was part of how the Club disguised the film participants. It was effective, I had to admit. She handed me a silver nightdress, gesturing at me to put it on. After I had slipped it over my head, she went to work on my hair, blowing it out into big, bouncy curls. A toxic blast of hairspray later, I was ready. She pointed to the door.

"Thank you," I squeaked, intimidated by her complete silence, and went back out onto the warehouse floor. Mr Green waved me over to one of the sets – a bedroom, dominated by a large four-poster bed.

"Looking good, Jade! You're gonna be just great. Now, hop up into the bed there, and I'll get set up."

I lay in the bed, on my side.

"Just roll over onto your back there, honey. That's great. Take your left arm up, onto the pillow. Fabulous! Head to the side... perfect! Now, close your eyes and get into the head space."

I did as he instructed. Even with my eyes closed, I could tell that he was adjusting the lights, making them brighter and darker. I focused on my role, over and over. I could feel myself getting turned on. It wasn't the camera and the filming that was exciting me, it was the unknown element. I didn't know how may men there would be, or what they would want me to do. I was starting to think that the hardest part would be pretending that I didn't want it to happen...

"Places, please. Going for a take. Remember your cues, guys – let's get this done in one!"

My cue was someone touching my clit. I wasn't to wake up until then. After that, I had no cues.

"And... action!"

I lay there, my eyes closed, trying to keep my face neutral and peaceful. I could hear a sound – the bedroom door opening stealthily. Creeping footsteps approached the bed.

"Well, look at this," a man's voice whispered.

"That's some sweet sugar right there," another one replied. "Do we have time?"

"Dude, we always have time for pussy," a third voice said.

"Think she'll be trouble?"

"I don't fucking care."

"Let's get a look at the goodies."

I felt the blanket slip away. I shifted slightly, but kept my position. It was hard to look so still when all of my senses were on red alert. I felt the delicate strap of the night gown slide down over my shoulder, exposing my breast. The set was cool, but that wasn't the reason why my nipples were rock hard. The other strap slid down, and I was topless. I kept on sleeping.

"Look at those titties. I bet, if you rubbed those titties just a little, that fucking slut would go off like a rocket."

My nightgown was slowly moving up, over my thighs, exposing my pussy.

"Fuck yeah, that's what I'm talking about. Watch this..."

A fingertip touched the very tip of my clit, so softly that at first I thought I was imagining it. But then it began to apply a gentle pressure, stroking ever so slightly. It was the only part of me that was being touched – without that, I wouldn't even know they were there. I moaned slightly, still pretending to be asleep.

"Is she wet?"

"Yeah she's wet, the fucking slut," came the whispered reply. "Bitch loves it."

The pressure increased slightly, and I moaned again, pressing my hips towards the finger. The only thing I was faking was the sleep – this was hot!

"Fuck this shit! Wake that bitch up," a new voice

said, louder and harsher than the others. WHAP! One of them had slapped my breast! I wasn't expecting that, and I gasped as my eyes flew open and I sat up. Four men were standing around the bed, and they were all wearing full face masks. It was a genuine shock. They were dressed in jeans and T-shirts, and each one had unzipped his jeans to expose a large, hard cock. I felt a thrill of terror.

"Who are you? Get out!" I said, my voice wavering.

"Shut the fuck up, bitch!" one of them shouted – the one with the harsh voice. He pointed a gun at me. "One word, one more motherfucking word, and I will blow your fucking head off!" He jammed the gun right up against my face. I felt the tears begin to flow. "Do you believe me?"

"Yes," I whispered. In that moment, I did.

He grabbed my hair. "Did you just speak, bitch? You don't speak, understand?" I nodded tearfully. "You do as you're told, and we'll let you go. Can you do that?" I nodded again, and he put the gun away.

"Seems the best way to keep the bitch quiet is to fill her mouth with something," one of them said. The others laughed.

"Me first, then," the man with the gun said. He seemed to be the leader. Still gripping my hair, he dragged me across to where he stood, so that I was kneeling on the bed in front of him.

"Open up, you fucking whore," he said, pressing the end of his thick cock against my mouth, "and suck it real good, if you know what's good for you."

As soon as I opened my mouth, he grabbed my head with both hands and rammed his cock all the way into my mouth and down my throat. He held it there as I choked and gagged, tears and spit flowing freely. Just when I thought I was going to pass out, he pulled back, allowing me to breathe. He started to thrust in and out of my mouth. I tried to suck him as well as I could, but he was moving too fast and deep for me to do anything but hang on for dear life.

"Hey, get me some of that," one of the others said, standing next to the first guy and pointing his cock towards me. Using my hair, the man with the gun started to move my head back and forth, so that I was impaled on one cock and then the other.

"Does she suck good?" a voice asked from behind me. One of them had moved around the bed. I felt him tear the nightgown that was bundled around my waist, ripping it off. I was naked now. The other man had joined the cock line-up, and now I was sucking three of them. The man behind me grabbed my breasts roughly, squeezing and twisting them.

"She sucks okay. Nothing special," one of them said.

"She has a tight little pussy, though," the man behind me said. He had moved one of his hands down to my clit, and I realised that this was the one that had been touching me earlier.

"She likes this shit," he said, rubbing me again.

He was right. I hated sucking their cocks – it was rough and violent, but his fingers on my clit were turning me on regardless. I could feel a fast, unstoppable orgasm building.

The man with the gun pulled my head back, away from the cocks.

"She's gonna cum, boys! The fucking slut is loving it!"

All three of them watched my face as I started to cum involuntarily, tears rolling down my cheeks.

"Oh yeah, this one's a whore!"

"She's had her fun. It's time for ours. Tie her up," the man with the gun said.

Two of the men dragged me about on the bed, fastening my wrists and ankles to the posts. When they had finished, I was face down, my knees tucked under me and my ass raised, completely exposed. I couldn't move at all. A gag was shoved into my mouth.

"You can scream all you want, now," a voice said in my ear.

"Okay boys, let's settle this. Who gets first pussy, who gets first ass?"

"I should get one of them, she didn't suck me off."

"Fine. Which one?

"First ass."

"I call dibs on first pussy!"

"First pussy is mine," a voice growled. The man with the gun.

I felt the mattress shift as he climbed up behind me. His hands gripped my hips roughly, and then without preamble he shoved his cock inside me, jackhammering in and out. I started to scream though the gag as he relentlessly battered me for what felt like forever. He pulled out without cumming, and another one replaced him. Fingers pushed into my pussy, scooping out the juices and working them into my asshole. And then a cock pressed in, slower than the other, but certainly not gently. He hammered away for a few moments, and then withdrew. The next one stepped up, and slid into my pussy.

"Her ass is tight, bro!"

He pulled out of my pussy and into my asshole, thrusting away.

"My turn now, Jesus!"

The last one took my pussy. He was thicker than the others, and he reached around my waist, touching my clit as he pounded me. It was no soft caress – he was pinching and twisting it. Through the pain, I realised that I was going to cum again. I let myself go, pushing back onto his cock and moaning though the gag. My body shuddered and my pussy twitched as I reached my climax.

"Oh yeah! This slut loves my cock!"

He carried on fucking me as one of them clambered onto the head of the bed and removed the gag.

"Suck it good, now"

I began to suck him, and immediately I could tell he was close to cumming. He groaned, pulling out of my mouth and stroking himself. Hot white ropes of cum sprayed all over my tear stained face.

"Looking good, bitch," he said. Immediately, he was replaced by another one. As I sucked him, I realised that the one in my pussy was close. He pulled out and spread apart my buttcheeks, exposing my gaping ass hole. I felt the hot liquid spatter my ass as he let go. The one in my mouth pulled out, coating my eyes and hair with his thick cum. Now there was only one left. The man with the gun. He climbed right up onto the bed, so that he was crouched over me. I felt his cock press against my tender asshole. He grabbed my hair and pulled my head back as he started to thrust.

"You like this, huh? You fucking whore. You want me to cum in your ass? Say it!"

"Yes!" I choked out.

"Yes what?"

"Yes, I want you to cum in my ass!"

He let out a guttural groan as he started to pump rivers of cum into my ass.

"Oh yeah, you fucking little whore," he said, sliding out of me. I could feel his cum trickling out of my hole and down over my pussy lips.

"We'll be back tomorrow."

He let go and climbed off the bed. There was silence for a moment.

"Annnnd..... scene!" Mr Green yelled. I jumped out of my skin – I had completely forgotten about him, about the cameras, about everything. I had been so wrapped up in the moment.

I could hear the men murmuring to each other as they moved away, but I was tied down so firmly that I couldn't move.

"That was fantastic! Honey, you're a star!" Mr Green enthused, as he began to loosen my restraints. "How do you feel? Good?"

"I feel great," I said. It was true, I did. I was shocked at how much I'd enjoyed it – the feeling of helplessness, of being the plaything of complete strangers. The danger, too. Although I had never been in any real danger, it had felt so real. I rubbed my wrists as I sat up and looked around. The other actors had disappeared.

"Well honey, you were perfect. There's a hot shower waiting in make-up for you, and your car's out front. You did good, kid." He winked at me, and returned to his monitors. Interesting, I thought. it seemed his kink was entirely based on the filming. He wasn't going to touch me himself. That was probably for the best – I don't think I could cope with his constant cheery enthusiasm. I was learning what I liked, now, and it seemed I liked it dark...

Quickly I showered, relieved to find that the tan washed away, dressed and headed out to the car park. I was so distracted that I even forgot to be embarrassed in front of the chauffeur. My head was filled with only one thing. The fifth challenge was completed, which meant that James was next. I hoped that Davina would be waiting for me when I got back to Belgravia – I really needed to talk about this. Luckily, she was.

"How did it go with Mr Green? Happy?" she asked.

"Yes," I said. "It was a, um..." What had he called it? "A home invasion scene. It was OK, really." I didn't want to tell her how much I'd loved it. I always felt that she expected a degree of professionalism from me. After all, the Prism Club was her job.

"How many men? They were masked, I assume," she said suspiciously.

"Four," I said. "Why?"

"You didn't notice, in the other films? There's normally five."

Now that she had pointed it out, I realised that she was right. Each film that Mr Green had made always featured five men, all with their identities disguised. Was it...

"The other billionaires," she confirmed. Sir Pink doesn't partake – he's not one for sharing – and obviously Mr Green is behind the camera, but traditionally the others join in."

I felt a moment of revulsion when I realised that the man with the gun had been the hateful Mr Yellow. But then, the numbers added up.

"One of them wasn't there, then."

Davina snorted. "No prizes for guessing who."

"But why? What does it mean? Is he dropping out?"

"It doesn't necessarily mean anything. It's his first year, so maybe he's just not into that, like Pink. Maybe he doesn't get along with the others..."

"Or maybe he doesn't want to see me again," I finished. My mind was torn. On the one hand, I felt rejected, but I was also glad that James hadn't been there. I wanted him, I realised, but not like that. Not just as another cock in a group.

"Well, if he doesn't, I haven't heard about it. This evening's report said that Green had cleared you, and Orange was next. Which means that we're going to have to talk about it – rationally, and without using the bloody word James," she said.

It was happening, then. I tried to be so many things – professional, nervous, even outraged that I would have to go through with it like nothing had happened. But all I could feel was excitement that I was going to see him again. I concentrated on looking nonchalant.

"Fine. Run me through it. What's going to happen with Mr Orange?"

"As I'm sure you remember, his scenario is a boss and secretary thing. You go to his offices – his real ones, so try not to make friends and influence people – and work for him. Lots of bending over, that type of carry-on. It's probably the easiest one, under normal circumstances."

It sounded like I'd be alone with him for most of the day, then, and away from the Prism Club, too. My heart leapt. At least I could apologise for how I'd treated him. Even if he still didn't want me, I'd feel better about that.

"Obviously," Davina continued, "you need to focus on keeping it professional. And not for his sake, either – I don't give a flying toss about him. For your sake. If he's nasty to you, or even just distant, you have to keep it together. He's not your boyfriend, he's just one of the members. Imagine how it would be with Yellow, or Blue. It could be exactly like that, and you'll still have to suck it up and smile, just like you did with them." She grabbed my hand, and I could see in her face that she really did have my best interests at heart. "You're so close to the finish line, and you can't imagine what that will mean for you. Your whole life will change forever. Don't screw it up now, over some guy."

"I won't," I promised, although the truth was, I really didn't know how I would react. Maybe it would be better if he turned out to be awful. It would be easier to forget about him, then.

"When does it start?"

"Tomorrow morning, nine am sharp," she said.

"Tomorrow!"

"Why not? You're not full of hormones this time, there's no reason to wait. Best to get it over and done with. And just think – it might be the last day of your life that you have to get up and go to work."

Tomorrow. That was...sudden.

"Now, get some sleep," she said. You'll get an alarm call at seven, the car will take you at half past eight."

"But... what about preparation – clothes and make-up?"

"You decide. He seems to like you as you are," she said dubiously. "I'm sure I'll see you at some point." She kissed my cheek, and got up to leave.

"Wait! What's my name for this one?"

"It's not bloody Elizabeth, that's for sure. Sienna is your name. And he is Mr Orange." Her voice was stern, but her eyes were twinkling. "Sleep tight."

Sleep tight? Fat chance. I laid in bed, but I was wide awake. All I could think about was what the morning would bring. At 3am, I jumped out of bed and sorted though my wardrobe, trying to decide what to wear. I must have tried everything on twice, before I settled on a grey dress. It was fitted and sleeveless, but long, right down to my ankles. It was made of some sort of soft wool. I checked the label – cashmere. It looked conservative enough for work, but it was the polar opposite of the naughty secretary get-up – no tight white shirt, short skirt, stockings-and-suspenders, high heels and glasses for me. I needed to feel self-confident to get through this if it went badly, and that could never happen in a glorified stripper costume. And also, I thought, I want to look like me. I might be pretending to be Sienna, but inside, tomorrow, I couldn't be anything but Elizabeth.

It felt as if I had finally closed my eyes only thirty seconds before the peal of the telephone shattered the silence. I lifted the receiver. It was Rose, the formidable lady I had met on my very first day. It seemed like a lifetime ago, now.

"Seven o'clock, Miss Sienna," she said, her cut-glass accent strident, even at this time in the morning.

"Thank you," I managed, before collapsing back onto the bed. God, I was exhausted. But in two hours, I would be standing in James' office. I had to get moving!

I blasted the shower on cold, and it did the trick. I was wide awake now, and I was filled with butterflies. I couldn't help it. Even though it might be awful – would probably be awful, I was excited. I got dressed, glad that I'd chosen my outfit last night. I could never have made such a decision this morning. I tried the dress on again, and it felt... right. Not right for the assignment, of course, but right for me.

I did my make-up simply, as Davina had taught me. With my new hair colour, I had to admit that I looked, well, good. It felt strange, and vain, to say that to myself. Usually, the sort of thoughts I had when I looked in the mirror were things that I wouldn't say to my worst enemy. But there was no denying, things had changed. It wasn't just the polish of new clothes and expensive cosmetics, either. It was me – I'd changed. I was more confident, somehow. Having handsome, powerful men desire me was part of it, of course, but it was also the experience of handling things, dealing with the different situations that I'd found myself in without falling apart. I was finally realising that I was somebody, a woman who could keep herself together and hold her own in a situation.

I could do this. I could handle whatever James threw at me, just like I'd handled all the others. I felt the nerves settle a little, although not enough to manage any breakfast. Before I knew where I was, it was half past eight, and the chauffeur was opening the Bentley door for me.

"Thank you," I said, looking him in the eye. I was invincible.

The offices were in a large block. Sixth floor, the chauffeur had told me. I stepped into the lift and looked for the right button. They were all labelled with a small, brass plaque. The one for the sixth was marked 'JMBlack Software.' That was his surname, then. Black. Funny that it was a colour. I wondered why he didn't use it as his Prism Club name, but I supposed it wasn't very discreet. And black wasn't in the rainbow, either. White was all the colours together, I vaguely remembered that from school. And black was the opposite of white, the total absence of colour.

I shook my head in irritation – my mind was rambling, when I needed it to be clear and focused. The lift had reached the sixth floor. The doors slid open, to reveal an open plan office space. There were a couple of people working at computers, but they didn't look up as I stepped into the office. I could see a door at the back of the room, leading to a second office. The plate on the door simply said 'Black.' The door opened, and there he was.

Immediately, my heart jumped in my chest. I hadn't seen him since the confrontation at the Club, when I'd screamed at him, and somehow in all that, I'd forgotten just how good-looking he was. He was wearing a suit – the first time I'd seen him in anything other than jeans and a T-shirt – and it made him look different, more powerful and commanding. He pushed his honey-blonde hair out of his eyes as he strode over towards me, his blue eyes carefully neutral.

"You must be Sienna," he said.

"Y- yes," I managed.

"Well, this is the main office," he said, turning and gesturing towards the room. "Doug over there, and Marcy..."

The two people, presumably Doug and Marcy, barely even looked up as they waved a hello.

"You'll be working though here, though, today," he said, starting to head back to his office. "Come through."

As I followed him, he paused at one of the desks, where a woman was typing away at a keyboard.

"She's new too," he said flatly. "You can ignore her, though. She won't be here long."

The woman looked up and smiled coolly. It was bloody Davina!

"Just keeping everything moving along smoothly, sir," she said. I pulled a 'what are you doing here' face at her, but she had already turned her attention back to the keyboard.

James opened his office door and held it for me, closing it softly behind us. We stood in silence, looking at each other. His neutral expression had disappeared when he closed the door, and he looked... conflicted.

"What now," he said softly.

"I don't know," I whispered...

SIENNA

I stood there, in James' office, staring at him. The last time I had seen his face, it was wearing an expression of hurt confusion, as I screamed at him in a hormone-fuelled rage. Now, it seemed wary and unsure. I realised that he was waiting for me to speak, to see how I would act. He was going to follow my lead.

All of Davina's instructions flashed though my mind, not least because I was very aware of her presence on the other side of the door, in the outer office. I just hoped the presence of the other staff – the real staff – would rein her in. Be professional. Be Sienna. Treat him like you would any of the others, I thought to myself. What would that look like?

I opened my mouth, fully intending to say something about the assignment, ask him what he wanted me to do, something like that. But that wasn't what came out.

"I'm sorry," I said.

"Sorry for what?" He was cautious, guarded.

"Sorry for... what I said. For shouting at you. Swearing at you. I was having a bad day, and I took it out on you. It's no excuse, and I apologise."

His face collapsed into relief.

"I thought you were telling me that you were quitting, for a moment there," he said, grinning.

I couldn't help it – the tears started. Quickly, he moved over to me, enveloping me in a massive hug.

"Shh, shh, it's okay," he whispered. "No harm done."

"I've- I've just felt really bad ever since," I sobbed into his shoulder. "I didn't know how to make it okay, and Davina said you might be awful to me, and I've been so worried, and-"

"Honestly," he said, looking me in the eyes and wiping a tear away with his thumb, "it's okay. Things are okay. We're okay."

And just like that, it was. I hadn't realised just how wound up I'd been about meeting James – meeting him as Mr Orange – until now. I'd been terrified that the connection between us was either broken, or had only ever existed in my head in the first place. But it was there, shining and real.

"I don't always cry," I said, as he handed me a tissue. He laughed, then glanced towards the door. Clearly, Davina was on his mind too.

"Come and sit down," he said, nearly whispering. "You know what they say about bats and hearing..."

He took my hand, and led me over to a small couch in the corner of his office. "She's not that bad," I said. "She's been a good friend to me, through all, well, this – the club and everything. She just takes a bit of getting used to."

"A bit of getting used to? After that first night, when I was in your room, she pinned me up against a wall!" he said, outraged.

"Really? She's half your size..." I said.

"Okay, not with actual pinning, but she glared a lot. She said that if I ever came near you again, she'd cut my balls off and have them bronzed."

"Yeah, I've been on the receiving end of the glare. I didn't know she'd spoken to you, though. She didn't mention it."

"What did she say? After I left? She seemed pretty angry."

"She calmed down soon enough. I think it was, well..." Part of me didn't want to tell him, and betray Davina's confidence. But on the other hand, I wanted James to see that she wasn't the evil harridan he thought she was.

"She was on the programme, and she kind of... fell for one of the bill- the men."

"The bill?"

I was embarrassed. "The billionaires. It's the term the club uses to describe you all. I never really thought about it until now, saying it to your face, but it feels like it's just defining you by your money. Like you're not really people, just wallets."

He laughed. "They call you the Penuries. I thought it sounded kind of sexy, until I looked it up. Penury means destitute. I guess they define everyone by their wallets." I blushed. It sounded like something a beggar would be called in the olden days. I wasn't a beggar, was I?

He stretched, reclining back on the couch. "So, Davina fell for a billionaire, did she? Who cracked her stone heart wide open, then?"

I leaned in against him, and he wrapped his arm around my shoulders. I could smell the citrus tang of his cologne. This was... nice. It felt so comfortable and natural, like we'd done it a thousand times before.

"The one that you replaced. That's all I know about him, apart from that it was years ago, and he didn't feel the same way. The club kicked her off the programme, but they offered her a job mentoring the new girls."

"So she had to work with him for years, setting him

up with girls? That must have been rough," he said thoughtfully.

"I suppose," I said. "She doesn't really like to talk about it. That's why she was so angry, though. She thinks the same thing will happen to me."

He picked my hand up, lacing his fingers though mine.

"It won't, though. Because I do feel the same way. If anything..."

His tone had turned teasing.

"What?" I said, laughing.

"It will go the other way. You'll reject me, and break my poor fragile heart. You'll leave the club, bugger off into the big wide world, and Davina and I will sit up together every night, getting drunk and bitter, talking about the loves we lost and what a cow you are..."

"I am not a cow!" I squealed. I turned to face him, grabbing his other hand and squeezing it, pulling his arms up above his head. "Say that I'm not a cow!"

"Oh yeah, this is straight out of the Davina School Of Charm, beating a man up in his own office." He was leaning right back, so that I was nearly straddling him. "It's a shame she didn't teach you how to defend against this!"

In one swift move, he grabbed hold of me and rolled off the couch. Now we were lying on the floor, James on top of me, face-to-face. Immediately, the mood shifted from teasing fun to pent-up lust.

"You're not a cow," he said, his pupils dilated. "You're-"

He kissed me, passionately. It was... amazing. Somehow, that one small act was more intimate, more sensual than anything I'd ever experienced, with anyone. I felt my whole body respond as I kissed him back, running my fingers through his thick hair.

He pulled back. "No, no. Wait. Stop."

"What is it?"

"I don't want... I don't want you to..."

"You don't want me to kiss you?"

"No, it's not that. I don't want you to feel like you have to. For the programme." His face was serious. "I'd rather that nothing happened between us, than something happened just for that. I'll tell them it was all fine in any case. Just... don't pretend. Please."

He looked so vulnerable.

"James," I said softly, stroking his cheek. "I'm not pretending. My biggest fear about today was that I knew I couldn't fake it, not with you. This is the real me, and the real you. No club, no games. Just us."

I watched his face relax, and then change again, into something else. Something wilder, and more passionate. The endless tension between us, the pressures of the club – it all fell away in a heartbeat. He kissed me again, hard and strong. I arched my spine, pressing my whole body against him as I fumbled at his belt buckle. The only thing I could think about was how much I needed him inside me. As I freed his cock, he was pushing my dress up to my waist.

"Are you sure?" he said, his fingers at my hip, twining around the delicate lace.

"Don't stop," I said, pulling his head back down towards me.

He tore my underwear away, and I gasped as he buried himself deep inside me. All the intricacies and pleasures I had been introduced to, and this simple act was better than any of them. Because it was him. I wanted to orgasm immediately, I wanted it to last forever.

"Oh god, Elizabeth," he murmured in my ear. "You feel so good."

He was kissing my face, my lips, my neck, and every thrust as he moved inside me was pushing me closer to the edge. I wrapped my legs tighter around his waist, pulling him into me, deeper and harder. I could hold back no longer. As the orgasm tore through my body, I felt him respond, his cock spasming as he pumped rivers of cum into me.

As the peak faded, our kisses became softer and gentler, until finally we were gazing at each other, flushed and smiling.

"That was..." I said.

"I know."

He looked at the scrap of fabric that was still screwed up in his fist.

"Sorry about your knickers," he said, grinning in a way that made me think he wasn't in the slightest bit sorry.

"Are you going to do that every time? Because I might have to place a bulk order," I teased.

"No," he said. "Next time, I will take off all your clothes, and all of my clothes, and fold them all up perfectly into a neat little pile, if you like. But this time, I just couldn't wait."

"Me neither," I said.

There was a knock on the office door.

"Fuck!" James hissed. He quickly fastened his trousers and pulled me to my feet, stuffing the underwear into his pocket. "I'm keeping these," he whispered, as the door opened. It was Marcy, one of his regular staff.

"The new woman said you weren't to be disturbed, but this contract needs your signature now, before the New York market opens," she said. James scrawled on the piece of paper she offered him.

"Is there anything else that's going to come up today? Anything that's so urgent?" he asked coolly.

"No," she said, glancing suspiciously at me. "You won't be disturbed for the rest of the day."

"Excellent," he said.

"It's fascinating, to see that side of you," I said, once the door was safely closed.

"What do you mean?"

"The businessman, in the sexy suit, giving orders," I said.

"Yeah? You think my suit is sexy?" he said, wrapping his arms around me.

"It's very James Bond," I said, nuzzling his neck.

He laughed. "Well, don't get used to it. If they don't need to disturb me, then I don't need to be here."

"What? You're leaving?"

"No, we're leaving. I'm not sitting in this bloody office all day with that old bat-"

I raised my eyebrows questioningly.

"-that lovely Davina out there spying on us and everyone else wondering what the hell is going on. Besides, it's nearly lunch time..."

"It's not even ten o'clock!"

"Do you want to stay?"

"Well, no..." I admitted. Getting out of here sounded perfect. "But what about, I mean, are we allowed?"

"I really don't give a fuck. We're not supposed to, no. If Davina tells, she tells – that's on her. But we," he grinned boyishly, all trace of the powerful businessman gone, "are playing hooky. Let's go."

"Bathroom first, though," I said. "I need to powder my nose."

His knowing smirk told me that he was fully aware of what I really needed to take care of – the steady trickle of cum that was creeping down my inner thigh.

"Through there," he said innocently.

In the privacy of the bathroom, I had a brief moment to panic. What was I thinking? Leaving the office, the designated place, and disappearing off into London would get us both in trouble – a lot of trouble. I knew he would agree to stay if I insisted, and we would still be spending the day together. But the truth was, I wanted to go with him. I wanted it to be just us – two people together without a care in the world. But you've followed every order the club has given, no matter how awful, my guilty conscience screamed. Why can't you just stay in the office? If you get kicked out, it will all have been for nothing!

But that wasn't true, I realised, and not just because of James. I had changed so much, come so far. I was more confident, more sure of myself that I had ever dreamed possible. And nobody could take that away from me. I was going.

"Ready?" James said, as I emerged.

"You have no idea how ready I am," I said, linking my arm through his. We stepped out into the main office.

"I'm done for the day," James announced. "Email if something disastrous happens, otherwise I'll see you all tomorrow."

Doug and Marcy barely looked up as they muttered goodbyes, but Davina leapt to her feet. I pointedly nodded my head towards Marcy as I met Davina's death stare. On my very first day, Rose Templeton – the programme recruiter - had told me that the Prism Club was founded on complete and utter discretion. I was using it against them, now. Davina couldn't say anything in front of James' office staff, and we both knew it. I felt a thrill of victory when she looked away first.

"Have a lovely day," she said tightly. "I'll be sure to email in the event of a complete disaster."

"How very kind of you," James said politely, steering me towards the lift.

As the doors closed behind us, he started laughing.

"She took that well," he said.

"Are you kidding me? She's furious," I said, giggling.

"She's just had a lot of Botox, that's all."

"That doesn't surprise me. She's very..." he trailed off, embarrassed.

"Very what?"

"Well, into her looks, I suppose. I'm not knocking it!" he said quickly.

"Then why are you looking so awkward?" I said, confused.

He actually blushed. "Well... you know... if you had – I'm not saying you have – it would be fine... and you look really nice..."

"For god's sake! I have not had Botox. Look!" I said, wiggling my eyebrows up and down at him. "Why would you even think that?"

The lift doors opened – we were in the basement car park. He took my hand and began to walk along the row of cars.

"I don't know! But you have the nails, and your hair is different, I thought maybe you might have had that as well." He stopped walking and turned to face me. He looked uncomfortable. "All of this... it's pretty new to me."

"What do you mean?" I said, squeezing his hand.

"I've not had loads of girlfriends. And since my work took off, there's not been any. I don't really know much about women and grooming and beauty treatments and fanciness."

I couldn't help but laugh. "You think I'm groomed and fancy?"

"You are!"

"I'm not. It's new to me, too." I kissed him. "And I hate the nails."

It was strange – part of me was pleased that he saw me as the polished, put-together woman I'd always envied, but a bigger part of me was relieved that he didn't think all women naturally looked like that. And if

I was being honest, I liked the bit about not too many girlfriends, as well.

"Come on, then," I said, starting to walk on.

"We're here," he said. "This is my car." I could tell he was trying to look humble and modest, but he couldn't fully disguise the pride in his face as he gestured at the vehicle behind him. I knew nothing about cars – I'd never owned one – but even I knew what an Aston Martin was.

"Wow," I said. "It's an actual James Bond car, to match your suit."

He opened the passenger door for me. "Get in, Pussy Galore."

It was impressive. The seats were soft leather, and when he started the engine, it sounded...powerful.

"Do you like it?" he said.

"It's... great. I don't really know much about cars, to be honest."

"I know what you're thinking," he said. "I swear, I'm not a flashy douchebag showing off my toys. But when I was a little boy, I got a model version for Christmas one year, and I always dreamed that one day I'd get a real one."

"That's sweet," I said, trying to picture him as a boy. "Who got you the model one?"

"My mum. It was just me and her, I don't have any brothers or sisters."

"It was just you and her?"

"Cancer, seven years ago," he said quietly.

"I'm sorry," I said. "That must be hard."

"I've learned to live with it," he said. "What about you, your family?"

"I don't have any, at least none that I know of," I admitted. "I was taken into care when I was a baby. I mostly grew up in children's homes. I had a couple of foster parents, but not long-term ones."

"That sounds rough, too," he said.

We were silent for a minute, but it was a good silence – companionable rather than awkward. I never usually told anyone about the way I grew up, but somehow it was just different with him. Easier.

James pulled out of the car park and onto the road.

"Where are we going?" I said.

"You'll see..."

As he drove, we talked about everything and nothing – our favourite TV shows, the music on the radio, the importance of adding milk to tea and not the other way round. "They're just animals!" James had said in mock disgust. We were far outside London when finally he turned off into a sleepy little village, parking up outside a pub.

"The pub? Sounds good to me," I said. I was secretly relieved that we weren't going somewhere posh and upmarket. This place was more my style.

"I like it here. The food's good, and it's..."

"Not a flashy douchebag place?" I finished.

"Exactly."

He held my hand as we walked in, and I realised that to the pub staff, we would just look like any other normal couple having lunch together. Like a boyfriend and girlfriend on a date. I liked it, but we couldn't pretend forever. The pub was lovely, and the food was great, but all too soon it was time to head back to London. As we climbed into the car, I couldn't hold back any longer. There was so much that I wanted to ask, so much that I needed to know.

"Why did you join the club?" I blurted out.

He grimaced. "Yeah, there's stuff we need to talk about, I know. But I didn't want to completely kill the mood. It's been such a good day."

"I know," I said, kissing him softly. "But it's time,

James."

He started the engine.

"I almost don't know why I joined, really. It's hard to explain. When my company took off, everything changed. I went from having nothing to having more money than I could imagine, practically overnight. And when it changed, everyone around me changed, too. Suddenly nobody was interested in me as a person, it was all about what I could do for them, what they could get out of me. I had women throwing themselves at me – women who wouldn't have given me the time of day a year earlier. It was flattering, sure, but I knew it wasn't me they were interested in, just my bank balance. Then I got talking to a guy at a party one night, who'd been there. He told me – in a very roundabout way, of course – about the club. He said it helped him."

"Which one was it?" I said.

"I believe you know him as Mr Purple," James smirked. "That's why he was so pissed off, when I carried you down the stairs that time. He'd vouched for me with the club, and there I was, breaking the rules..."

A thought occurred to me.

"You met him at a party?"

He laughed. "A professional business function, not an orgy. That's not really my thing."

"What is your thing, then?"

"I'm getting to it," he grinned. "Respect the narrative flow!"

"I'm sorry, please continue with your story," I said, laughing.

"Yeah, so, he told me about the club, and what it involved. It seemed – I don't know – honest, I suppose. Everyone is clear about what they're offering, and what they're getting out of it. And for my own part, I felt that being around all that kind of stuff, money, rich people, power – it would help me get used to it. Because it doesn't feel real. I can wear the suit, I can drive the car, but all the time I still feel like an imposter. Like I'm still the poor IT nerd who can speak Klingon but can't talk to girls."

I was amazed. He always seemed so confident, so sure of himself. I had no idea what was going on beneath the glossy surface of his life.

"Your turn. Why did you join the club?"

This was the question I'd been dreading. I didn't want him to think that I was just another gold-digging whore – because I wasn't – but I could see how it would look to anyone else. I wasn't sure how to start. Should I reassure him I wasn't interested in his money? That's probably what they all said. Instead, I told it to him as it had happened. That way he could make his own mind up about me.

I told him about how my life had been before. Not just about being an unemployed virgin with no prospects, but the emotions of it – the way I'd felt so invisible, so alone, so worthless. I told him about the perfume, and the interview, where I'd been asked the fateful question – what do you have to lose? It had never been about money, for me. I'd joined the Prism Club because I had known deep down that I couldn't live my entire life out the way it had been. Something had to change.

"If an army recruitment brochure had have fallen out of that magazine, instead of a perfume advert, I'd be wearing camouflage and saluting right now," I finished. "But it didn't."

"Do you wish it had? Something different, I mean. Something other than the club."

I thought about it for a moment.

"No, I don't. It's not all been great, but it's been important. I've changed so much. I'm not afraid any more. I know I can make my way through life on my own."

"Do you want to? Be on your own?"

I took a deep breath. It was time to take the risk, put my cards well and truly on the table.

"No. I want to be with you," I said softly.

He was looking straight ahead, at the road. His face was a mask. The silence stretched out agonisingly.

"Good," he said. "That's what I want, too."

He glanced over at me and smiled.

"I'd kiss you now, obviously, but I don't want to romantically drive us into the back of a lorry."

"It's OK," I said. "You can kiss me later." I squeezed his thigh.

"Oh, I plan to do much more than that," he said, grinning.

"Such as?" I teased.

"Well, you asked me what my thing was. So, we're headed back to the office. It would be a shame to let all that programming go to waste..."

When we got to the office, things were quiet. Doug was still tapping away at a keyboard, oblivious to the cleaning lady attempting to polish his desk. Davina and Marcy had left. Although it appeared Davina had not gone quietly – there was a note on James' desk, addressed very pointedly to Sienna.

"I guess this is you," James said, handing me the envelope.

I'd barely even thought about my name this time. With the others, it had helped me embrace the new persona, but with James it was simply pointless. I could never be anyone but Elizabeth with him. I opened the note.

Elizabeth – I'm hoping you get this tonight, before you return to the club. I don't need to tell you that your actions today were completely insane, as I'm sure you already know that. And there's no point in me harping on about it. What's done is done.

I do understand, darling, really I do. I've only tried to discourage you from this path because I know where it leads, and not just for you. If the club find out about today, they won't just ask you to leave. They'll ask James to leave too. When a girl leaves on bad terms, the club is unconcerned. They have the money and the power to deal with her, if she decides to go public. If a member leaves on bad terms, though, it's a different story. There will be consequences for James.

I've seen the way he looks at you, and there's no doubt in my mind that he cares for you. You need to make sure that he doesn't make some foolhardy, macho stand against the club. Come back to Belgravia tonight as normal, and we will speak in private about what to do next. But for God's sake, don't let him do anything rash.

D.

I read the note twice, trying to absorb it all. I looked at our names, our real names, in Davina's spiky handwriting, and I felt guilty about the way I treated her earlier – as if she was only a club employee. She was my friend, and she was on my side. She was being careful, in the note, not to say too much, but the implications were clear. If I didn't play this right – if we didn't play this right – the club would destroy James.

"What does it say, Elizabeth?" James asked.

I looked at him. He was still wearing the suit, although he had loosened his tie. His honey-blond hair was tumbling down into his eyes, and the beginnings of a 5 o'clock shadow were appearing along his chiselled jaw line. The note had scared me, and I didn't know what was coming next. All I knew was that I wanted him, and I needed to take every opportunity that I had to be with him. Until all this was over, there were no guarantees.

"Well," I said coyly, "it wasn't addressed to Elizabeth. It was addressed to Sienna. Had you forgotten about her?"

He smiled evilly.

"You know, I almost did. I've been so distracted by my new girlfriend, Elizabeth, that I barely had any time to pay attention to my lovely secretary."

"Oh yes? Lovely secretary, is it?"

He nodded, grinning.

"Tell me more," I said, moving towards him.

"When I had planned this originally, of course, it was going to play out slightly differently. I didn't know you back then, and I wasn't even sure if I'd want to fuck whoever they sent. And I'd assumed, of course, that the girl would be wearing some sort of god-awful sexy secretary outfit. So we'll have to improvise a little. Go and sit out at the desk opposite Doug, and turn the monitor on."

Interesting. I hadn't known what to expect, but I'd thought that I would at least be in the same room as him.

"Oh," he said, as I opened the door to the main office, "it's an ergonomic chair. Spinal health is important." Something about his wicked grin told me that he wasn't being entirely honest...

I went over to the desk. The chair – well, it wasn't really a chair at all. It was more like a horse riding saddle, but slimmer. It reminded me of something a hairdresser would use. I looked around – all the other desks had similar chairs, although mine seemed to be made of a different material. I perched on the chair and turned the monitor on. Immediately, a message flashed up.

-Not like that. Sit so that the chair is underneath the dress.

I looked up. The door to James' office was open, and

he was sitting behind his own desk, staring at his own monitor with a carefully neutral expression. I sent a message back.

-*What about Doug, and the cleaner?*

He was typing on his keyboard, still not looking at me.

-*I don't think you'll fit Doug and the cleaner up there.*

-*Haha. What will they think?*

-*Doug won't notice. I could fuck you on his desk and he wouldn't notice. He's a very meticulous employee. The cleaner will just think that you don't want to get your dress creased. A lot of women sit on those chairs that way, I swear.*

I stood up slightly, and quickly flicked the dress down over the chair. Straddling it like this, after losing my underwear that morning, meant that my bare pussy was pressed against the vinyl fabric. I frowned as a thought occurred to me.

-*How many women have sat on THIS chair, with no knickers on?*

He was still looking at the screen, but I could see a smile playing around the corners of his mouth.

-*Nobody has sat on that chair before. It's new. Now do some work.*

-*What work?*

A file opened on the screen, behind the chat window.

-*Just some basic personal assistant stuff. It's all in the file. Just call the numbers, place the orders, make the arrangements.*

-*Okay...*

I opened up the file. I was half expecting the orders to be crazy sex stuff, but it was exactly as he had said. I quickly scanned through. There were instructions for a dry cleaners, he wanted his car servicing, ordering business cards – nothing out of the ordinary. Was this his thing, knowing that I was sitting on his weird chair with no underwear? Although, he had thought that I would be wearing a slutty secretary outfit. A short skirt would have to be hitched right up to sit on a chair like this. Maybe he had a stocking fetish. I almost regretted choosing something tasteful instead – it would have been exciting to see him excited. But the rest of the day had been worth it. I picked the phone up and called the first number.

"High Street Dry Cleaners," a bored voice said.

"Yes, hi," I said, nervously. I'd applied for hundreds of receptionist jobs over the years, and never got hired. Clearly, it wasn't something I was good at. I quickly read the instructions on the screen. "I'm calling from James Black's office, regarding an order. It was supposed to be delivered to the offices yesterday, and it doesn't seem to have arrived."

That was it. That was all the information on the screen.

"It will be there tomorrow. Or the day after," the bored voice said. I felt a flash of annoyance.

"Well, which one? Not that either is acceptable. You agreed to have it done by yesterday."

"I don't know," the bored voice said.

"So go and find out!" I snapped. The tinny music in my ear told me that I had been placed on hold. I waited impatiently. But as I sat, I began to feel something. At first, it was so subtle that I thought I was imagining it – in fact, I thought that I was so annoyed at the dry cleaner that I was shaking with rage. But it wasn't me. It was the chair. Silently, discreetly, it had begun to vibrate. I looked at James. He was still staring at his screen, not looking at me.

The vibration was getting stronger. I could feel my pussy getting wet as the vinyl hummed against it. I knew that my cheeks were reddening, and it was a struggle to control my breathing, and keep it normal. As it increased, it was harder and harder to act like nothing was happening. I wanted to grind myself against the chair, to ride it. But I couldn't – I couldn't do anything apart from sit there as the vibrations got stronger.

"Miss?"

Shit! I hadn't even been thinking about the phone call.

"I understand that you are calling from James Black's office. I'm the manager here. I'm terribly sorry about the delay - it seems that there has been a glitch in our system. If you can give me the address of your offices and your order number, I'll have your items biked over first thing in the morning."

I could barely speak, I was so close to cumming.

"One moment please," I gasped, pressing the mute button on the handset. Immediately, the chair stopped vibrating. I looked over at James. His face was a picture of innocence – which was the dead giveaway. James never looked innocent.

I released the mute button. Still staring at the screen, James reached out and clicked his mouse. The chair started vibrating again. I pressed the mute button, James clicked the mouse again and it stopped. So, that was his game…

I released the mute button again, taking a deep breath as the chair burst into life.

"Mr Black is a regular and valued customer of yours. I'm sure you can find his details in your system. Good day."

I slammed the receiver down, and the chair stopped vibrating.

-Cheater. It should have taken you a good ten minutes to find the order number to give him. How do you like the chair so far?

-It's very… ergonomic.

-The original plan was to do this all day. You've

probably got time for one more phone call, though.

I glanced at the clock – two minutes to five. Doug and the cleaner seem to be wrapping things up. I dialled another number – the business cards order. I figured that it wouldn't matter as much if I messed up this one, rather than the car servicing appointment.

"In Design Printing."

"Hi, I'm calling to place an order for some business cards," I said, hesitantly. I was waiting for the chair to start vibrating again, but it didn't. I looked at James. He was furiously clicking the mouse...

"No problem. You have an account number?"

I gave him the number on the screen. The chair was still not vibrating.

"Design reference code?"

Again, the information was on the screen. And again, the chair did nothing. I couldn't help myself.

-Want me to make a call about the chair, after this one? I think it's broken...

"Thank you madam. If you could just read out the text to me, I'll input it and read it back to you."

I scrolled down to the information. Bloody hell.

"I'm sorry about this," I said. "It seems to be all in French. My French isn't great."

"Me neither," the man said. "Say the words first, and then say the letters, too. It will take longer, but we'll get there."

I glanced over at James again. He was smiling, presumably in anticipation of my horrible language skills. Doug was shutting down his computer now, preparing to leave. Awkwardly, I started to read the incomprehensible words on the screen. A message flashed up, interrupting my struggle.

-Ooh lala! Very sexy. An accent like that could give anything the horn.

This time, James was looking right at me. He raised

his eyebrows as he theatrically clicked the mouse once more. The chair was moving again, but this was different. It wasn't vibrating at all. Instead, something was pressing against the lips of my pussy, slowly but surely sliding its way up inside me! My eyes widened in shock.

"Madam? What comes after homme?"

In a daze, I read the next couple of words out, spelling them without being asked. The thing in my pussy seemed to be some sort of dildo – a mechanical cock built into the chair. It started to move up and down, filling me each time. The chair was fucking me. I tried to sit completely still, but it was almost impossible. Finally, Doug put his coat on, waved goodbye, and accompanied the cleaner into the lift. Thank God. There was still the man on the phone, but at least I could move now.

I leaned forward onto the desk, shuddering as the cock pumped into me. Between clenched teeth, I muttered the last few items of text into the receiver.

"Okay, let me read that back to you," the man said cheerily.

A hand reached out across the desk, deftly pressing the mute button and the speakerphone button at once. Hesitant French, even worse than mine, began to fill the room.

"Looks like you've got until our boy here finishes," James said, standing over me. He bent down and pulled my dress up, dragging it over my head and tossing it onto the floor. He unhooked my bra, and then I was naked – straddling the seat as it pounded me. It was amazing and incredible, but I still wanted him inside me. His cock was straining against his trousers as I unzipped him. I ran my tongue slowly along the underside, trying to torment him, like he had tormented me. But my lust and desire was too strong.

I took him fully into my mouth, sucking his length as

hard as I could, matching the pace of the machine. He was groaning, running his fingers through my hair as I sucked his cock. I was starting to orgasm, moaning through my stuffed mouth as my body shook and spasmed.

As it subsided, James pulled his cock out of my mouth. Quick as a flash, he pulled me up, off the chair, and spun me around so that I was bending over the desk, face down. He pressed the entire length of his body against me, kissing my neck, biting my earlobes, the weight of his chest along my back. He pushed into my pussy, bigger than the dildo, stretching me deliciously. His breath was in my ear, harsh and ragged, and I knew he was seconds away from cumming.

"Is that the order, madam? Are you happy with that?"

I stabbed the mute button, leaving the speakerphone on. Now, the man could hear both of us.

"Can you just check the account number for me again, please?" I said politely.

James buried his face hard into my neck as he started to cum, his hands gripping my wrists as he filled me with his load. I could feel him shuddering as he desperately tried to remain silent. When I was sure he had finished, I reached out and hung the receiver up, ending the call.

"Oh you bitch," he gasped into my ear, covering my cheek in kisses.

"Ha! Serves you right," I said, wiggling around until I was facing him, wrapping my arms around his neck. "You were planning to give me a full day of that – I think I'd have exploded by lunchtime. You'd have had to take me back to the club in a bin liner."

His smile faded a little.

"Yeah, the club. You need to be getting back there soon. The car's waiting outside. But..."

"But what?" I said.

"What are we going to do about that? I feel like a dick saying this, but I hate the idea of you going ahead, seeing the last guy."

I sighed. I hated the idea too, but there was more to it than that.

"Let me up," I said, "you need to read Davina's note."

His expression darkened as he read Davina's words.

"What does she mean by consequences for James?" he said.

"I don't know, I thought maybe you would. Did they not say anything when you joined, about leaving?"

"Not like this, with all this bad terms shit. They made it sound like guys only leave if their circumstances change – if they get sick, get married, get bored of it."

He crumpled up the note in his fist.

"I don't give a fuck. We decide, not them."

"I don't want to do it any more," I said. "That's not even a question. I only want you. But I can't make a decision without knowing the consequences. I need to talk to Davina, and find out how to handle this. I'll see her when I get back. Come to my room later, and we'll decide."

"Okay," he said reluctantly. "At least that way, we know what to expect from them. But you don't have to do a single thing that you don't want to do. Not for them, not for me, not for anyone. You know that, don't you?"

"I know," I said.

I wrapped my arms around his waist, nuzzling his neck. I only knew one thing, in truth. He was the only man in this world that I wanted, and I was damned if anybody was going to hurt him.

CORAL

I looked up at the building in front of me. 10 Belgrave Avenue, Belgravia, London. It was arguably one of the most exclusive addresses in the world. It had been the home of the Prism Club for over a century, and more recently, it had become my home, too. I'd changed so much, since I came here, and all of it for the better. I should be grateful, I knew that. But I wasn't. I was afraid. I'd been afraid before, of course, but this time was different. I had been scared for myself, scared of the experiences and what they would mean. But now I was scared for James, not myself. And it was the Prism Club itself that was scaring me. Leaving him behind at his office and returning here had been almost physically painful, but it had to be done. I took a deep breath, and opened the door.

Davina was waiting for me in my room. I wasn't surprised, not after what had happened – James and I disappearing, the mysterious note she had left me. I braced myself for the tirade, but to my surprise it didn't come. As I watched her pace up and down, I realised that she was as afraid as I was.

"Did you handle James?" she said.

"Yes, I mean, I think so," I said, sitting down. Her pacing was making me nervous. "He's not going to do anything or say anything, if that's what you mean."

"He doesn't want you to do the last assignment though?"

"Of course not, no. But I haven't decided – we haven't decided – on anything at all. I wanted to talk to you first. The note you left wasn't exactly crystal-clear," I said. "And for god's sake, sit down. You're making me seasick."

"Okay, this is how I see it," she said, sitting on the bed. "If the club find out about this – this thing – between you and James, we're all for the high jump. At the moment, they don't know anything. The Mr Orange report was fine."

"What did he say about me?" I asked, fascinated.

She raised her eyebrows sardonically. "Nothing. I wrote it myself in his sodding office, while you two were out gallivanting. Honestly, I don't know how he looks at those people all day. I was so tempted to pin that Marcy down and take my tweezers to her. But anyway," she said, "that's beside the point."

I was amused that even in the midst of a crisis, Davina could still take time out to be horrified by less than perfect grooming. I knew better than to show it, though.

"Now," she continued, "you need to decide. If you see the last one, and it goes well, then you're done. You can ask for whatever you want, or even ask for nothing – just a favour down the line somewhere. James can say that the club wasn't what he was expecting, and resign his position. Once his resignation is accepted, you can officially be together. Happily ever after, etcetera etcetera."

"But what if I don't see the last one? What then?"

"That's going to be… more difficult. You personally, of course, are free to leave at any point. You'll leave with nothing, but that's not the issue. The club will let you go, but they will look into why you left. And to be this far in and quit, they will focus their attention on the most recent assignment – James. I've covered up what I can, but these people are relentless. They will dig and dig until they get to the truth."

"The truth?"

"James has broken the rules. They don't take that lightly, not at all."

"The consequences that you mentioned? Is that what you're talking about? What will they do?"

"I don't know exactly – it's certainly never come up before, not during my time, but I looked back through the archives, and I read some of the contracts. They will ruin him. Not just financially, either. The power these people hold is unbelievable. They could have him branded a criminal, have him locked up in prison for the rest of his life – anything at all. If you can imagine it, they have the ability to do it."

It was ironic – that was the sentiment that had brought me here in the first place, that had convinced me to let the Prism Club change my life. I had never thought about what life would be like with the club working against you, instead of for you. I was horrified.

"That can't happen," I whispered. "That's… that's terrible! He's done nothing wrong. We've done nothing wrong."

"I know, but that's not how they'll see it. These aren't normal people – they're obscenely rich, powerful men who are following rules that were laid down a hundred years ago. If one of the girls breaks the rules, they don't care, because they barely see her as human."

"James said they call us the Penuries," I remembered.

"Really? The stuck-up twats," she said, offended. "Anyway, they don't take it personally. If one of the members, however, breaks the rules, it's different. This is one of their own, someone equal to them. They see it as a sleight, an insult to their power and control. Alpha male bullshit, basically."

I was quiet for a moment, letting the implications of what she had said sink in. I didn't need to consider my options – there were no options. Either I took the last assignment, or James was destroyed.

"I have to do it, don't I?" I said.

"Yes," Davina said bluntly. "There's no other way. You've managed the others just fine, though. It's just one more. How do you think James will take it?"

"I don't know," I said. "He doesn't want me to do it, and he knows that I don't want to do it, either. I don't think he's going to love the idea of me doing it for him."

"That's understandable. He's going to want to take his chances, fight his own battles. But you can't let him – because he'll lose. You'll both lose."

She was right. He had to let me do this.

"When is it? The last one?"

"Tomorrow."

"Tomorrow! That's not enough time to think, to prepare. It's too soon," I gasped, horrified.

"I know. I deliberately moved it up the schedule. The last thing you need is time to think. You just need to get it over and done with."

Her tone became slightly sarcastic. "I'm assuming loverboy will be paying you a visit later this evening?"

"Sometime in the night – once everyone's asleep," I admitted.

"Good. You can tell him then, and he won't have enough time to dwell on it and do something stupid. James deciding to throw himself on the sword will end in disaster, even if he's doing it for the right reasons."

"I know," I said. "It's the best way. What about all the rest of it? Preparation and so on - the assignment stuff."

"There's not really anything to do. It's at his house – his mansion, actually – and the car will pick you up in the morning. He doesn't really care about what you look like, how you are presented, any of that. You are called Coral, he is always called Sir, and do whatever he says. It's as simple as that. I'll see you when you get back, and we'll open a bottle of champagne." She moved towards the door.

"Thank you," I said. "Not just for this, for everything. You've done so much for me. You're a good friend." I leapt to my feet and hugged her tightly.

"You're welcome," she said. Her eyes were red rimmed.

"Are you crying?" I said teasingly.

"I'm trying to," she said. "New fillers. Just wait till you're my age, you'll understand. I'll go and put the champagne on ice, ready for tomorrow. Try not to stay up shagging all night, won't you? It will be no fun to me if you're asleep in the chair."

"I promise," I said, smiling.

After she had left, I got ready for bed. They didn't seem to be much point in doing anything else – I didn't know what time James was coming, just that it would be very late. Staying up and worrying about things was a bad idea. I knew what I had to do, and the last thing I needed was to talk myself out of it. I turned the lights out and crawled under the covers, and in no time at all I had drifted off.

I was woken by a pair of strong arms wrapping around me, pulling me to his bare chest and spooning me.

"Hi," James whispered into my ear.

"Hi," I whispered back. I could feel his hard cock,

barely grazing my bottom. I shifted slightly, pressing myself against it. His hand was resting on my belly, so I covered it with my own, sliding down between my legs.

"Mmmmm," he murmured, kissing my neck as he stroked my clit. His fingers moved up and down, tracing my lips, dipping inside me before returning to the tiny bud of nerves. It was slow, delicate and excruciatingly erotic. I was soaking wet as he moved his hips, pressing the head of his cock against my pussy. He kept stroking as he slowly pushed into me, filling me up.

"Does this feel good?" he whispered.

"Amazing," I breathed. It was. I felt as if my senses were on fire. As he moved inside me, ever so slowly, shivers of bliss flooded through my body. He started to pick the pace up, grinding deeper into me, his breath in my ear becoming more ragged.

"Faster, harder," I begged.

He started to thrust, now, his fingers drumming against my clit. It was ecstasy.

"Oh god, oh god," he moaned.

I reached behind me and grabbed his hair, twisting my fingers through it as I started to orgasm.

"Don't stop," I managed, as wave after wave of pleasure crashed through my body. I could feel him cumming inside me, the hot liquid spurting from his shuddering cock, pushing me to further heights.

"I'll never stop," he whispered...

We laid in silence for a while, just holding each other. Neither one of us wanted to break the spell, and crash back down to reality. But I could feel my eyelids growing heavy, and I knew I had to tell him. I just didn't know how.

"This is nice," I started.

"Yeah, it is," James said. "It's about to get less nice, isn't it?"

I sighed. "Davina was waiting for me when I got

back."

"How was she? Is the old bat going to grass us up?"

"James!" I said, elbowing him. "She's not an old bat. And she's my friend, she's on our side."

"On our side against whom, exactly?"

"The club. It's...it's bad. If I leave now, they'll investigate, and they'll find out about us, and then they'll come after you."

"I'm not afraid of the club," he said. "They're just old men with too much money and delusions of grandeur."

"That's the thing, though! It's not delusions. They will destroy you, she said."

"I don't care! It's just money – it means nothing to me," he said. "You don't want to carry on, right?"

"No, I don't want to, but-"

"Let me finish. So, you don't want to do it. I don't want you to do it. If you go ahead and do it anyway, just so that they don't destroy me, what does that make me? I'm not that guy, Elizabeth. The money, the business – none of it is worth that. I couldn't live with myself."

"It's not just the money, though. It's everything. They can have you arrested, thrown in prison for the rest of your life."

"For what?"

"For anything – pick a crime! You know who they are, the kind of access they have. You wouldn't get a fair trial, even if you got a trial at all. And is it worth that? A life sentence? Thirty years in prison?"

I could see the anger in his eyes. "I can't let them control me, Elizabeth. I don't want you to do it. I don't give a fuck what happens to me."

"But I do! I give a fuck! I don't care about the money either – if anything, it terrifies me – but I don't want you to get banged up for the best part of your life. How am I supposed to live with myself, visiting you in prison every week for the next thirty fucking years, knowing that I could have avoided it all by doing just one small thing. And it's not just for your sake, either. It's for my sake, too. Think about what I'd be losing, spending the next three decades waiting for you." I was trembling with emotion – frustration, fear, sadness and anger whirling around inside my mind.

His face softened as he looked at me.

"You'd wait for me?" he said softly.

"Yes," I said.

"For all that time?"

"Yes."

"Even though it would mean being alone, never getting to have children, never having any real sort of life?"

"Yes," I said. "I would."

"I love you," he whispered, his voice strangled with emotion.

"I love you too, James. And that's why I'm going to do it," I said.

"But-"

"No. No buts. You have to find a way to be okay with this. Because I only have two options – doing it, or being a prison widow for the next thirty years. Surely, you can see that doing it is the lesser sacrifice." I said.

He was silent for a moment. I stroked his hair, waiting for him to speak. He couldn't talk me out of it, and I knew he could never be pleased about it, but I wanted him to accept it, at least.

"Fine," he said, finally. "I understand, I do. I hate it – I absolutely fucking hate it – but I understand. You're not just doing it for me, you're doing it for yourself, too. There's one condition, though."

"What's that?" I said.

He grinned, kissing me on the nose. "All our children are being called James."

"What?" I said, laughing. "All of them? Even the

girls?"

"Especially the girls." He started tickling me.

"How many are we having?" I screeched.

"Loads. Thirty. One for every year I'm not in prison. That's the condition. Do you accept?"

"Yes! Stop tickling me! We can have thirty children and call them all James!" I said, trying to grab his wrists to stop him.

"Then fine, I give you my permission to go," he said, rolling on top of me and kissing me. "When is it?"

"Tomorrow-" I looked at the clock. "No, today. It's today, now."

"Jesus, that's fast."

"At least it's over with quicker. By the end of the day, we'll be free and clear of this place."

His face was solemn. "We will be."

"You should go, though. It's nearly morning. We just need to hold it together and get through today," I said.

"I know. I'll be here when you get back," he said.

"What will you do in the mean time?" I asked.

"I don't know. Go to the office, and brood a lot, probably. I can't stay here all day, I'll end up killing someone."

"It will be over before you know it," I said, kissing him. "Now go!"

He was all I could think about for the rest of the morning. After I had finally managed to shove him out of the door, the sun was coming up and there was no point in going back to sleep. Not that I could have slept, anyway. I was so excited. I loved him, and he loved me, and we were going to spend the rest of our lives together...

I got dressed, ate my breakfast, and got into the car. One more journey, and then I was done. I pushed the thought of what would happen today out of my head. I would do what needed to be done, but only with my body – not my mind. On all the other assignments, the ones before James, I had embraced them fully, opening my mind and my heart to the experience, but things were different.

In a way, I reflected, I would be like the women I had met working at the brothel. They didn't care about the men they slept with, I had learned, in fact they barely even noticed them. It was just a job, a means to an end. That was the mentality I adopted as the Bentley swept me deep into the countryside. All that mattered was the clock – hours and minutes counting down to freedom. I would let this man, this Sir Pink, do what he wanted with my body, but in my mind I would be with James, warm and safe and happy.

Eventually, the car turned up a long, meandering driveway. We had arrived. The house was enormous – an estate, really – and the chauffeur guided the car around the elegant building to a side entrance.

"You're to go through there, Miss Coral," he said politely. "Follow the corridor along to the end, and then through the double doors."

"Thank you," I said. He turned to get back in the vehicle.

"Wait," I said. "What time are you picking me up?"

I had never asked anything like that before, never queried what was happening, but I had to know how long it would be, exactly, before I was finished.

He looked surprised.

"I haven't been asked to pick you up, Miss," he said.

"Why not?" I said. "Will they ask you later? Or is someone else bringing me back?"

"I really wouldn't know, Miss Coral," he said, backing away. "Good day."

Well, that was frustrating. I knew I'd be back by

evening time, as Davina was meeting me for champagne to celebrate, but I would have liked to know exactly when. I wanted to go back in the Bentley, too. The peace and quiet would enable me to push everything out of my head before I saw James again. Never mind, I thought. Every day ends, and this one will too. The Bentley was already at the gate, moving at a terrific pace. He normally waited until I had gone inside – clearly I'd mortified him by my questions. I opened the side door. The sooner it began, the sooner it would be over.

I had entered a long, wide corridor. There were many doors off to each side, and I had a moment of panic – then I remembered that the chauffeur had said to go through the double doors. Only one entrance, the farthest one, had double doors. I made my way hesitantly down towards them, feeling like an intruder. This place was even posher than the Club. Portraits lined the walls, and as I looked I could see resemblances between each face. This was clearly the kind of house that was passed down from generation to generation over the centuries. I was no art expert, but judging from the clothes depicted, some of the paintings were hundreds of years old.

The thick carpet muffled my steps, and I realised what was so strange – the silence. I couldn't hear anything at all, any sign of life. A house this grand must have a sizeable staff to maintain it, but there was nobody around at all. It was unnerving me, and I tried to brush the feeling aside. What do you want? I told myself irritably. A meet and greet? A cup of tea in the kitchen before you go and fuck their boss? I was more confident than I had been, yes, but I wasn't that confident! I had reached the double doors. Should I knock? I thought. Yes. Anyone who lives in a place like this, and insists on being called Sir at all times will expect me to knock. The sound of my knuckles on the wood made me jump, seeming so loud in the quiet. There was no answer from within. I knocked again – still nothing. Maybe there was nobody behind the doors, just instructions or something. I opened one of the doors and stepped though.

"You just came in."

A man was standing in front of a large fireplace, his back to me. He didn't turn around as he spoke. Was he Sir Pink? I couldn't tell. He was wearing a navy suit, and his hair was palest blond.

"Sorry, I... I knocked but there was no answer. I wasn't sure what to do," I said.

"I didn't ask you a question," he said coldly. "I made a statement. In this house, you speak only to answer questions, when I ask them. In this house, when you reply to those questions, you use the honorific 'Sir', to denote that you are aware that you are speaking to your betters. And in this house, you do only what you are told – no more, and no less."

Jesus Christ! I knew it was just a game, just a roleplay, but still – it was going to be tough getting though the day without answering back. I hadn't even seen his face and I already disliked him.

"Do you understand?" he said.

"Yes, sir," I said, trying to keep my tone polite.

"Better," he said, turning to face me. I was surprised – he was far older than I had expected. His hair wasn't blond, it was white with age. His skin was leathered and wrinkled, his lips thin, and his eyes cruel. The thought of touching him repulsed me. So what? I scolded myself. Would you have preferred it if he was a model? It was true – I'd have been repulsed anyway. He wasn't James, and that was all that mattered.

The old man glared at me.

"Put that on," he said, jerking his chin towards a pile of clothes stacked on a small table. Mechanically, I walked over and picked the fabric up. It was a maid's uniform – barely. The neckline scooped down to the waist, and the frilly skirt part was no more than a couple of inches long. I longed to ask if I should keep my underwear on, but he hadn't asked me a question. Besides, I already knew the answer.

I stripped off – efficiently, not sexily. I knew I should probably be making more of an effort, but I just couldn't bring myself to do it. I glanced quickly at him as I stepped into the maid dress, trying to gauge his reaction. He was watching intently, and there was a gleam of something in his eyes, but he didn't seem aroused, exactly. The dress fitted, but I felt naked. My breasts were completely exposed, and my bottom half was barely covered. If he were sitting, he'd be able to see everything.

"Pick up your old clothes and your shoes," he snapped. I did as he said, slipping my shoes off and adding them to the pile in my arms. There were no others provided, so I waited, barefoot, to see what he would tell me to do next.

"Throw it all into the fire," he ordered, stepping away from the fireplace. Was that going to be part of it? I would have to go home like this? I silently prayed that he wasn't planning to send me home on public transport. I'd be arrested for indecent exposure, and that was if I was lucky. If I was unlucky...

I threw the pile of clothes into the flames. They weren't mine, anyway. They belonged to the club.

"Very good," he said. "They are no longer serving a purpose, so they should be disposed of. That's the right thing to do, don't you agree?"

"Yes sir," I said. I had no idea what he was talking about, but agreeing with him seemed to be the safest option.

"Yes, the right thing to do, indeed," he said, moving over to a cabinet. "For example, look at you. You're behaving yourself now, but at first you were insolent. It would be wrong, unfair even, to give you the impression that insolent behaviour can be washed away by respectful behaviour. That's simply not the case."

He took a riding crop out of the cabinet. So, that's what he's into. It wasn't entirely new to me – Mr Red had spanked me with his hand, and with Mr Purple, I'd used a leather whip on a woman. I knew the pleasures that a little pain could bring.

"You must be punished, for your own benefit," he continued. "Don't you agree?"

"Yes, sir," I said. The sooner it begins, the sooner it's over.

He walked over to me, the crop in his hand.

"Maybe there's hope for you yet..."

He was fast – I didn't even see it coming. The whip bit into my cheek, hard.

"...but I doubt it," he finished.

I stared at him, gasping, as blood dripped down my face and onto my bare breasts. There was not an ounce of pity in his cruel, merciless eyes.

I'm in real trouble here.

"Follow me," he said, turning on his heel and walking away. Shaking, I walked behind him, my head down, not looking where I was going, not looking at anything. I was in shock. He was still holding the whip, and as I followed him, I could see a drop of blood – my blood – drip onto the carpet. Something was very, very wrong. This wasn't the club's way.

He stopped walking, and I looked up. We were in a small room, a TV room, it seemed. There was a small leather couch, facing a large black screen. He sat on the couch and patted the seat next to him invitingly, raising his eyebrows in encouragement. I wasn't that stupid. I stood rigidly, my hands at my sides, trying not to clench my fists.

"You are a fast learner, I must say. Sit down next to me."

He didn't seem disappointed, or even pleased, that I'd realised he was trying to trick me. He just seemed...neutral, and somehow that was even more terrifying.

"Do you like watching porn?" he said.

I wasn't sure what to say. I'd barely seen any, outside of Mr Yellow's films, so I could hardly call myself a connoisseur, but I had enjoyed it.

"I- I'm not sure, sir," I stuttered.

He stared at me for a moment, as if trying to decide if he was pleased with my answer or not. Then he turned away, picking up a remote control and pressing buttons.

"I don't really bother with it myself, to be truthful. A young man's game, in my opinion. Of course, when I was a young man, a chap would be lucky to get his hands on a grubby magazine, let alone the videos they have these days. If I were young today – goodness! I'd be like a dog with two bones..."

It was bizarre. His tone was friendly and engaging. He sounded like any other kindly old man, reminiscing about his youth. Was he mad, or was it another trick? The screen flashed into life. A video was loaded up, paused. I couldn't tell what it was – the image on the screen was dark.

"Sadly, I'm no longer an young man," he said. "That's why I didn't bother partaking in the film you made. I do hope you're not offended. Are you offended?"

His eyes were wide, as if the idea of offending me was terrible to him. As if he hadn't cut my face open minutes earlier.

"No, sir," I said. Was he going to play the film I made? Let him - I really didn't care.

"Good, good. If I were a young man, of course, I'd have jumped at the chance. You do understand, don't you?" He seemed so...nice.

"Yes, sir," I said.

"Any young man would jump at the chance, don't you agree?" he said kindly.

"Yes, sir," I said. I was almost beginning to doubt myself. Had he just not realised he'd hit me so hard?

"And yet," he said, his tone turning to ice, "one young man didn't."

I was paralysed with fear. James had turned down the video. It was before we were together, after we'd argued. With everything that had happened between us since, I hadn't given it a second thought.

"Why do you think that is?" he said. All traces of friendliness were gone now, and I could see it had all been an act. This was his true self.

"I don't know, sir," I said.

"In my experience, when a man turns down guaranteed pussy, it's usually because he's getting it somewhere else," he said. "You were with James Black all day yesterday, were you not? For your scheduled appointment?"

"Yes, sir." My mind was racing. How much did he know? Was he just suspicious, fishing for information? I had to deny everything.

"And did you... fulfil the requirements of the appointment?"

"Yes, sir," I said. The report Davina had forged had said as much.

"Interesting. He was able to, well, perform, then? As a man?"

"Yes, sir." Did he think James was gay, or impotent? That would explain why James would turn down performing in the porn film.

"So tell me, truthfully. Do you know where, outside of your appointment of course, James Black has been sticking his dick?"

I swallowed. "No, sir."

He pressed a button on the remote, and the video started playing. I could see the image clearly, now. It was James and me, last night, in my bed. I could feel the blood thundering in my ears. On the screen, I begged James not to stop as I wrapped my fingers into his hair.

"So, either he drugged you, which would make him a rapist, or you're a liar. Which is it?"

"I- I'm a liar," I mumbled. I could barely think, my mind was racing so fast. The video had sound – he knew everything.

"Yes, you are," he said. "And you will be punished, of course."

I flinched as he raised the crop.

"Oh no, not this. What you've done is far more than mere insolence. I'll have to give it some thought. It's important that, moving forward, you don't do it again."

He stood up, and moved towards the door.

"Enjoy the show," he said. "I'm afraid you'll be watching it alone, though. I have things to do. I need to make my report to the Club. They've no idea what's been going on, you see. I made my enquiries...privately."

I felt sick. It was all my fault – I never should have allowed James to come to my room. We'd spent the whole together, and that should have been enough.

"Oh, don't worry about your little friend," he said. "I could tell them everything, yes. And you were right – they would completely and utterly destroy him. But what good does that do me? None. I'm going to tell them that it was all too much for you. You broke down in tears, sobbing on my shoulder. Being a kindly man, I didn't want to see you with nothing, so I gave you a few thousand pounds – enough to start a new life, somewhere far away. They'll scoff, behind my back – there's no fool like an old fool – they'll say, but they'll believe me. And I'll get a new servant. I do have the damnedest trouble keeping staff – I can't imagine why."

I leapt to my feet.

"I'm not going to be your fucking servant," I spat.

"That, of course, is entirely your choice. I explained how things work in this house, though – you serve a purpose, or you burn..."

He stepped through the door, slamming it behind him. I tried the handle – locked.

Fuck! I paced up and down the small room. There were no windows, no other doors, no phone. I was trapped. As I paced, I tried to calm down, tried to tell myself that he was only trying to scare me. But deep down, I knew he was being deadly serious. It all made sense – the chauffeur, with no orders to collect me, the eerie silence in the house, the burning of my clothes and shoes – items I could have escaped in. I had to make a plan – but what? I didn't know what was going to happen. All I could was wait and see.

I sat down on the couch. On the screen, James was tickling me, talking about how many babies we would have - I couldn't watch it. I reached for the remote control. No. Fuck him. I launched myself across the room and ripped the power cable out of the wall. But he'll punish you, a voice in my head said. I recognized it immediately – it was the old me, the one that had come to the Club. Obedient and scared of her own shadow. But that girl was gone, now.

I tore the other end of the cable out of the TV. Now I was holding a cord, a couple of feet long. I wrapped it around my waist, the only place I could conceal it under the ridiculous dress. I would wait and see, yes. But sooner or later, an opportunity would present itself. And I would be ready to fight back...

It was hours later, when he returned. That was a mistake. I had nothing to do but sit and think, and as I did, I had become angrier and angrier. My temper had raged and boiled, passing though the red-hot, fiery stage into something else. A cool, calculated fury. I was no longer fire – I was ice.

I composed my features as I heard the lock click. He would expect me to be terrified and hysterical, so that's what I needed to be. Not to please him – I was done pleasing people – but to lull him into a false sense of security. I sat on the couch, eyes downcast, trembling.

"I didn't tell you to turn the TV off," he remarked. He didn't notice that the cable was missing. I made a muffled sound, as if I was about to speak but had then thought better of it.

"I brought you your supper," he said. "As it's your first day. You'll be making all the meals from now on, of course. Do you like sandwiches?"

What kind of a fucking question is that? I thought. Who doesn't like sandwiches. Dick. It was all I could do to not laugh in his face.

"Yes, sir," I said meekly, staring at my bare feet.

"Good." He placed a tray down on a small side table and waited. Did he think I would go over, without permission? He'd already played that card once. I looked up – and that was what he was waiting for. He unzipped his trousers and pulled out his wrinkled, flaccid cock. A jet of piss arced out, over the sandwiches. He was watching it, moving his cock back and forth so that every inch of the bread was soaked. My hand crept behind me, under the woefully inadequate skirt, and found the cable. I began to pull at it, wrapping it around my palm until I had it all.

The gush of urine had stuttered to spurts, and then, it seemed, he was finished.

"Eat up," he said, smiling coldly. "All of it. There will be no wasted food in this house."

I got to my feet, my hand still behind my back.

"And what do you say?" he asked.

I smiled widely. As I did, I felt the cut on my cheek open again, chasing away the last remnants of fear.

"I say thank you," I said, beaming. I shook my hand, releasing a foot or so of cable. He looked at it, his cold contempt turning to something else. Fear? Rage? Regret? I couldn't tell. I didn't care.

"Thank you, for your hospitality. I've really had a marvellous day. But I must be going, now," I said.

"You're going nowhere, you little bitch," he shouted. I lashed out with the cord, and it hit him across the face. I slashed it again, but this time he managed to grab the end of it. He started to pull, trying to tear it from me.

"You're going to pay for this, mark my words! Such insolence! You will know your place!" he thundered.

"Her place is with me," James said from the doorway. His gun was pointed directly at Sir Pink's chest.

"Get down on your knees. Do it!" he snapped. His face was white with anger. Sir Pink let go of the cable and shuffled down to the floor.

"You okay?" he said, his eyes fixed on the old man.

"Fine," I said, stunned.

"Tie him up with the cable," James said to me. "Try anything, you old shit, and I'll blow your fucking head off."

With trembling fingers, I tied Sir Pink's wrists behind his back, fastening the knots over and over. I didn't know what I was doing, but it seemed secure enough.

"It's done," I said, standing up.

"Let's go," he said. I moved to his side.

James finally looked at me. I was suddenly embarrassed, remembering the degrading outfit I was wearing. But that wasn't what he was staring at.

"Did- did he do that to your face?" he said thickly.

"Yeah," I said, my fingers rising involuntarily to the cut on my cheek. It was still bleeding from where it had cracked open.

His mouth was a hard line as he strode over to where Sir Pink was cowering on his knees.

"You motherfucker," James said, and punched him in the face. Sir Pink bonelessly collapsed to the floor, unconscious.

"We need to go, now," he said.

I grabbed his hand and together we ran through the huge, silent house.

"How- how did you know," I gasped.

"Escape first, questions later," he panted, flinging the side door open and sweeping me up, over his shoulder. He ran across the gravel, opening the passenger door and depositing me into the seat, before tearing the driver's door open and jumping in. The engine roared, and half a second later we were flying though the gates.

"I can't believe you're here," I said, still breathless from the running, the shock, the whole thing.

"Pleased to see me?" he said, grinning.

"Yes! Talk about the nick of time!"

"You seemed to be holding your own," he said.

"James, what was that? How did you know?"

"Hang on," he said, turning down a country lane. "We need to get off the main road. There's a bag on the back seat with some clothes. I'm not saying I don't like the dress, but it's very...conspicuous."

I reached around in the seat, and found the bag. It was a sports bag, filled with clothes that seemed to have been stuffed in hurriedly. Some of the things were mine, from the club, but some of them were men's clothes. James' clothes.

"We're not going back, are we?" I said.

"We can't. Get dressed. I can't explain it all if your tits are looking at me."

As I pulled on a jumper and some sweat pants, he pulled the car over. We were in the middle of nowhere. I managed to find a pair of trainers at the bottom of the bag.

"Tell me," I said.

"You first. What the hell happened?" James said.

I told him everything, about the camera in my room, about Sir Pink's plan to make me vanish from the radar. "He said he wasn't going to tell on you, though," I said.

"He lied," James said grimly.

"How did you know? About everything?" I asked.

"It was Derek who tipped me off. He came to the office, and said he was worried about you."

"Who's Derek?" I said, confused.

"The chauffeur! Derek the chauffeur," James said.

"Oh. I didn't know his name. He was worried about me? And went to your office? He always seems so...professional."

"He keeps his mouth shut, that's what he's paid to do, but he sees everything that goes on, and he's a decent bloke," James said. "He'd been told that you were leaving the club for good that morning, so when you asked him about being collected, he knew something was up."

"How did he know to come to you?" I asked.

"He said, and I quote, 'I didn't want to bother Miss Davina, 'er having such a temper on 'er, and Miss Elizabeth was like a moony-eyed cow when I picked 'er up from 'ere yesterday, so I thought you ought to know'. Those were his exact words."

"He doesn't talk like that!" I said, outraged.

"He does. He can 'please' and 'thank you' with the best of them, but he grew up in Walthamstow."

I was so shocked, and touched. I'd barely said two words to him – I was always ashamed, worried that he was judging me. But he'd been watching me, looking out for me, this whole time.

"I should thank him," I said.

"Elizabeth, you don't understand. You'll never see him again. We can never go back, not to the club, not to London. After he left the office, I called Davina. She checked the system – the bastard had filed a report saying that you'd quit and gone up north. There was something else, too. My resignation letter. The one I had planned to give them tonight. I knew right then that we were both fucked."

"Jesus," I said. "What are we going to do?"

"We're going to run. Maybe before, if you'd just quit, it wouldn't have been that bad. I'm sure I'd have been a model prisoner. But now... I don't think they'd stop at jail time. So, I told Davina to pack you a small bag of essentials, and bring it to the office."

"Davina packed that bag?" I said incredulously.

"No, she packed two suitcases and something called a 'look book'. I grabbed a couple of things and shoved them in with mine. But anyway, while I waited, I made some phone calls. I've managed to get us fake IDs. They won't hold up for any length of time, but it should be enough to get out of the country."

"We're going to the airport?"

"No, too conspicuous. We'll take the ferry to Rotterdam, and from there – who knows? I managed to get enough cash to keep us going for a few months, maybe even a year or so if we're careful. We can sell the car, but without papers we won't get much for it, I'm afraid. Although..."

He looked uncomfortable.

"Although what?"

"You don't have to. It's me the club will be looking for, not you. Davina said you can stay with her."

"Don't be ridiculous!" I slapped him on the arm. "I'm coming with you."

"But you need to think about it. What kind of life can I offer you? We'll have to stay off the radar forever. We'll never be able to get passports, never be able to come back to the UK. And we'll be dirt poor."

I kissed him.

"We'll be together, though. And that's all that matters."

"You're sure?" he asked.

"Completely," I said, smiling. "Let's go."

"I should probably get rid of this," he said, opening the window and tossing the gun into a ditch.

"Is that safe? What if a kid finds it?"

He laughed as he started the engine. "It's a cigarette lighter! I'm not actually James Bond, you know."

He wasn't. He was James Black, and he was all mine...

ELIZABETH

All of that happened three years ago. When I think about it now, it hardly even seems real. The club, the money – it's another world. The first year was tough, moving from place to place, sleeping with one eye open. But the second one was better. We found a small, ramshackle farmhouse in rural France. The owner didn't ask too many questions, and was happy for us to pay the rent in cash. We settled in, and made it a home.

I began to tutor the local children in English, and found it improved my atrocious French considerably. James started his own business, helping pensioners with their computers. It doesn't bring in the kind of money his last company did, but it's enough to keep us in baguettes and vin.

After we'd been here a year, we had our first visitor – Davina. She had resigned her position at the club the day we left, and with ruthless Davina efficiency, forced Mr Purple into giving her a job as the fashion editor for one of his glossy magazines. There were no club reprisals for her – she knew too much.

She had come in person to tell us the news. The club were no longer actively looking for James and me. Sir

Pink had died, and he had been the driving force behind the club's desire for retribution. As long as we didn't return to London, we were safe.

"You can go anywhere," she had said, as we drank wine in the garden after dinner. "New York, Paris..."

"We're going to stay here," I told her.

"But why?" she asked.

"We like it," James replied.

She looked around, with ill-disguised horror. A chicken was pecking at her handbag, and she snatched it out of harm's way. "But why?"

Being safe from the club meant something else, though. Two days later, we said our vows at the local chapel, with Davina as our witness. She had threatened me with terrible violence if I cried and ruined the perfect make-up she had applied for me, but in the end we had all shed a tear, even her.

That had been a year ago, and she was due to visit again soon. She'd had emailed me that morning, to inform me of her visit and remind me to 'get rid of those pestilent birds' before she arrived. I heard a car outside – James' Aston Martin. It was the one thing we had kept, the one souvenir of our old lives. It had been his childhood dream to own one, and I couldn't bear to see him give it up, even though he'd offered many times, when money was tight.

"Davina's coming next week," I called out, as he opened the door.

"Really? I thought she hated the countryside," he said.

"She does," I said, heaving my massive bulk out of the chair and waddling over to kiss him. "But she says we're not fit to dress a French baby, so she's bringing a few items..."

The End

ABOUT THE AUTHOR

Lena Foxworth lives in England with her crazy cat, Pudding. She enjoys writing romance nearly as much as she enjoys reading it.

Look out for her next work – Manchester Bad Boys, a series of three novellas set in Northern England.

www.lenafoxworth.com

Printed in Dunstable, United Kingdom